TOMORROW'S PROMISE

Lara is determined never to risk falling in love, but when she takes up a new teaching post, finds it isn't quite so simple. She shares a house with fellow teacher Mick, whose laid-back manner hides a warm heart that threatens to melt even Lara's cool exterior. Trying to distract herself with a spot of property development only seems to involve her in endless problems, which Mick is more than happy to help resolve. But should she let him?

GILLIAN VILLIERS

TOMORROW'S PROMISE

Complete and Unabridged

LINFORD
Leicester

First published in Great Britain in 2009

First Linford Edition
published 2010

British Library CIP Data

Villiers, Gillian.
  Tomorrow's promise.- -
  (Linford romance library)
  1. Teachers- -Fiction. 2. Love stories.
  3. Large type books.
  I. Title II. Series
  823.9′2–dc22

ISBN 978–1–44480–455–3

Published by
F. A. Thorpe (Publishing)
Anstey, Leicestershire

Set by Words & Graphics Ltd.
Anstey, Leicestershire
Printed and bound in Great Britain by
T. J. International Ltd., Padstow, Cornwall

This book is printed on acid-free paper

A New Beginning For Lara

I have to get this job, I just have to, thought Lara as she hurried along the unfamiliar road. And then, calm down. Stop being so melodramatic. She did want the job, desperately, but if she wasn't offered this post she would find something else. Wouldn't she? One way or another, she was going to move on.

She tried to think positively, to get in the right frame of mind for the interview. She had the qualifications and experience needed for the teaching post. She had an excellent reference from her previous Head of Department. Remember how motivated and hard working she was.

And yet the doubts crept in again. None of these things counted if they didn't want her. The last few months had taught Lara it wasn't enough to be good at what you did, other people had to value you too. And if they didn't, if they really wanted to drive you down, it was so hard not to go under.

She felt a small rush of relief when she finally found her way to Loreburn High School. It was one of the ugliest buildings she had ever seen. This was a good sign. If it had been a pretty building, she would have known it wasn't meant for her.

She hesitated before the wide metal gates. Take a deep breath. Check that the train journey and the walk hadn't given her that crumpled look she so hated. Remember what Alex had said about smiling. OK, ready to go.

'Are you lost?'

Startled, she swung round to find a man standing almost at her shoulder. Where had he sprung from?

'No, I'm not lost, thank you,' she said. 'I'm looking for Loreburn High School, and it seems to me that I've found it.'

'So you have.' He grinned. He was about her height, wearing extremely scruffy sports gear, and standing rather close. 'You'll be here for the interview?'

'As it happens, I am.' She looked at him more closely, wondering how he knew. He couldn't be a teacher here, could he? With his untidy blond hair and wide smile he wasn't at all like the teachers she was used to.

'Best of luck,' he said, patting her lightly on the shoulder, making her jump.

'Thank you,' she said stiffly, and marched across the empty playground towards the unattractive buildings.

It was only when she got closer that she realised she couldn't actually see a way in. The school was a series of concrete boxes of different heights, with courtyards and passageways between them, but she couldn't see any signs of an entrance. She chewed her lip. If she wasted any more time she was going to be late. She turned around to ask directions from the stranger, and saw him jog lazily around the corner to the playing fields.

OK, another deep breath. If she kept walking she was bound to find a door eventually. She felt hundreds of pairs of eyes watching her from the expanse of windows. She straightened her back and tried, at the same time, to look relaxed. She could do this. Really, she could.

★ ★ ★

The interview went better than she had dared to hope. The interview panel were pleasant and interested, keen to put her at her ease. Lara felt silly for having worked herself into such a state, but none of that mattered now. Mr McIntyre, the head teacher, asked her to wait after the question-and-answer session had finished, which she hoped was a good sign.

It was. When he called her back in, he offered her the job there and then.

'I'll quite understand if you want some time to consider. In the meantime, would you like to have another

4

look around the school buildings, meet some of the other teachers . . . ?'

Lara smiled properly for the first time in weeks. It was as though the weight of the world had dropped from her shoulders. Yes! The first step towards her new life had been taken.

She was going to like her new head teacher. A wiry, energetic man in his early fifties, he was straightforward and friendly. She answered him in the same way. 'I'm sure I should think it over before I give you an answer, but I think you can take it I'll say yes.'

'Excellent, excellent. And you said you could start after the February half term break, is that right? You don't need to work out any notice?'

'No, I gave in my notice a while ago.' He didn't ask why and she didn't explain. Lara didn't want to think about her old job.

'Wonderful. So we'll see you here a fortnight on Monday. Which brings me to the next point. Accommodation. Have you thought of anywhere to stay?'

'No, I . . . '

'You didn't want to jump the gun. Quite understand. But we aren't giving you very long to get organised, are we? I happen to know that one of the other teachers has a room to let in their house, and I wondered if that might be of interest to you? Short term, of course, but it's convenient for the school and no doubt preferable to a Bed and Breakfast.'

'That's very kind of you.' Lara was impressed. When she had taken her job in Glasgow nobody had shown any interest in her living arrangements. 'I'll certainly think about it.'

'Very good.' Mr McIntyre was back on his feet. 'No time like the present, eh? I'll take you through to the staff room, see if I can introduce you to Mick right now.'

Lara knew, she just knew, as soon as they walked into the sprawling, noisy staff room which of the twenty or so teachers would be the one with the room to rent. She was sure this wasn't a good idea. She wanted to say something to Mr McIntyre, but he had already cleared his throat and a silence of sorts fell.

He introduced her as, 'Lara Mason, who I very much hope will be our new Senior Geography teacher.'

Then he led her across to the far corner where two men were sitting with mugs of coffee, their feet on a low table, watching her approach. They were both wearing tracksuits and one of them was the man who had accosted her at the gate.

'Mick Jensen, Sandy Woods. Let me introduce Lara Mason. Mick, I told Miss Mason that you might be able to help her with accommodation.'

Mick pushed the too-long, sunbleached hair from his eyes. 'We've already met.'

'Excellent. Well, if you'll excuse me . . . ' Mr McIntyre patted Lara's shoulder in a fatherly fashion. 'I'll see that letter goes off to you straight away.'

And then she was left alone in the

room full of strangers.

'So you got the job,' said Mick Jensen. 'I knew you would. Congratulations.'

'Thank you,' said Lara, doubtfully. Somehow this man seemed to be laughing at her and it made her uncomfortable.

'Would you like a coffee?' asked the other man. He was older and tidier than his colleague.

Lara smiled at him. 'That would be lovely. White, no sugar.'

He rose in the fluid movement of the very fit and went to a kitchen alcove. Lara hesitated, waiting for the man called Mick to invite her to sit down. When he didn't she said, 'I'll have a seat, shall I?' Really, did he have no manners?

'Help yourself,' said Mick easily. He gestured with his mug to the numerous empty chairs, and then, apparently making a supreme effort, lifted his feet from the coffee table. 'What brings you to this part of the world, then?'

He had a way of looking at her as though his whole attention was caught, green eyes wide and interested, and just a little amused.

'I'd heard it was a good place to live,' she said cautiously.

'It's not bad. Know the area at all?'

'I've visited. One of my friends has family nearby.'

'And where are you working just now?'

'Glasgow.' She named the school.

He grinned. 'Aye, I can see why you'd like to get out of there.'

'It's all right.'

'You'd be too lah-di-dah for those kids.'

'I'm not lah-di-dah.' She didn't know why he riled her so much. It didn't matter what he thought, after all. He would never know it wasn't the children who had been the problem.

Sandy Woods came back with the coffee and she turned with relief to accept it.

'Where is it you're from?' asked the

9

older man, his tone friendly.

'I was brought up partly overseas. Saudi Arabia, Kuwait, various places.' Lara had therefore spent years at boarding school, but she didn't mention that. It hadn't been a happy time.

Sandy asked Lara a few more questions then rose saying, 'Time I was off. I'll let you two talk about arrangements.'

'You've not changed your mind then?' Mick bent down to rummage in the massive bag at his feet and pulled out a packet of chocolate digestives. 'Want one?'

'No. Thanks. Changed my mind about what?'

'Moving to Loreburn. I hope we haven't put you off.' He began to eat his way through the packet, speaking between bites. 'D'you want to hear about my house? It's a couple of miles away. It's nothing special. Three bedrooms, but one's little more than a boxroom, so it's really only two. I've been renting out the second room to help with the mortgage. We share the bathroom, kitchen, etc. Split the bills. What do you think?'

'Why did your last tenant move out?'

Mick said, 'He couldn't stand the chaos, of course. No, actually, he's bought a place of his own. He'd always meant to do it, but being Steve it took him a couple of years to get round to it. He moves out next week, which leaves me in the lurch.'

'If I did take it, it would only be for a short time,' said Lara cautiously. 'I'd really like to get a place of my own and I don't intend to take a couple of years over it. Perhaps you'd rather look for someone who would rent longer term?'

Mick put another biscuit in his mouth and she had to wait a moment before he answered. 'Not a problem.' He smiled. 'You look like the perfect housemate to me.'

Lara could feel herself blush again and resented it. 'I don't know . . . '

'And you're probably a much better cook than Steve, too. No, only joking, I don't expect you to cook for me, or me for you, unless it suits. So, are you interested?'

'You haven't mentioned the rent yet.' Lara really wanted to say No. There was something about this man with his laid back manner and inquisitive eyes that disconcerted her. But when he mentioned an amount that was half what she would have paid in Glasgow, and she thought of the convenience of having a solution offered to her on a plate, she weakened.

'I haven't officially accepted the job yet, but if I do, and you're sure . . . '

'No pressure. Think it over and you can give me a ring.' He delved into the enormous bag again and came out with a crumpled notepad. 'Have you got a pen handy? I'll give you my number.'

Lara passed him her favourite fountain pen, at which he gave a silent whistle, and she watched as he wrote out the information in a surprisingly attractive script. He handed her the piece of paper but kept hold of the pen, turning it over in his hand. 'Nice. I suppose you want it back?'

'You suppose right.'

'Bit fancy, though. Isn't it a hassle filling it in with ink and all that?'

'It's a hassle I consider worthwhile.'

'Are you a school teacher or something?' he said with a grin. 'Do you want to come over and see the house now?'

'No. I . . . ' Lara glanced at her watch and noted with relief that she could honestly say she had to catch her train. She wanted time to think things over, away from this man. She had never been one to make decisions in a hurry. She still couldn't quite believe she had given in her notice in Glasgow without another job to go to.

Taking risks wasn't like her at all, which just showed how desperate she had been. She shuddered. She was not going to think about that now. 'I'll phone you in a few days' time,' she said.

'I'll look forward to it.' He swung his feet back on to the table and popped the last biscuit into his mouth.

It was as she was walking briskly back to the railway station that Lara saw Ladybank Row for the first time. On the way to the school she had been far too preoccupied to notice her surroundings, but now she was free to look about.

It was good to be back in Loreburn. The small town feel, even on a grey January morning, was comforting. Yes, it felt homely and peaceful, just as she had remembered.

Then she glimpsed the higgledy piggledy broken-down houses and wondered why she had never noticed them before.

She had five minutes to spare and, after a moment's hesitation, she turned down the little cul-de-sac. The houses stood on one side of the street. On the other was a fence hiding a small industrial estate. Behind the houses was a line of trees and Lara thought she could glimpse a railway line beyond them. What a funny little spot this was.

Then, as soon as she turned into the little road, it was as though she was miles from the town centre. The traffic noise faded as the great bare trees nodded to her. And there was a sign standing askew in the front garden, For Sale.

She went closer, interest kindled, and then saw the words *As One Lot*. That was a shame. Those funny little houses with their pointy roofs and oddly-placed windows had a strange appeal. But buying one place so run down would be a challenge, a row of four was out of the question. Lara was nothing if not sensible.

She turned on her heel and headed back to the station.

Lara Makes Arrangements

Elizabeth Mason was surprised, and very pleased, to receive a phone call from her daughter. They spoke, dutifully, once a week, but it wasn't usually Lara who initiated the calls. Elizabeth could understand that, overseas calls were expensive. It made it all the more exciting to receive a call now.

'Lara, darling. How are you?' Elizabeth settled herself down on the white settee close to the air-conditioning unit. The weather in Dubai was even hotter than usual.

'I'm fine, thanks. And how are you and Dad?'

Elizabeth answered cheerfully, suppressing a sigh at the formal way her daughter spoke. How could it be they were so far apart? Not just the hundreds of miles, but the coolness between them. Not for the first time she wished they hadn't

16

had to send Lara back to the United Kingdom for her schooling. But there hadn't been any choice, had there? They had moved around so much with Derek's work, it was important to give the child some stability. Lara had always been a child who longed for stability.

'Mum, I've got a new job.'

'Goodness! Have you really? Why, we didn't even know you were thinking about changing jobs.'

'Didn't I say? Well, things weren't going so well at school since that new Head of Department started, so I thought I'd look for something else.'

A wave of sadness swept Elizabeth. Lara had been unhappy and they had known nothing about it. She tried to be positive. 'And have you found something nice?'

'I've got a job at a school in Loreburn. I'll be moving down there in a few weeks time.'

'Loreburn? Gosh, that is a big change.' Lara had seemed so settled in Glasgow. 'Why Loreburn?' Elizabeth wished Lara had discussed this with them first. Derek was coming up for retirement and it would have been lovely if they could all move somewhere a little closer together.

'Alex's gran used to live near Loreburn, don't you remember? I've always liked the town.'

Elizabeth vaguely remembered Lara had spent some holidays with her friend, Alexandra, in a town in the south of Scotland. It hadn't always been possible for her to fly out to the Middle East. But she hadn't realised her daughter had liked the place so much. In fact, she had never quite understood the friendship Lara had with Alex, a plump quiet girl who had none of Lara's verve. There was no time to go in to that now. Instead she concentrated on the practicalities. 'What will you do with your flat?'

'Sell it, of course, and buy somewhere down there.' Lara sounded impatient. 'The Headmaster of the school seems really nice, he's arranged for me to rent a room off one of the other teachers whilst I look for somewhere to buy.'

'That's kind. Is she your age?' Elizabeth would like to think of Lara sharing with someone of her own age. Apart from Alex, she didn't seem to have any close friends.

'It's a man, actually.'

'O-oh.' Elizabeth couldn't keep the disapproval out of her voice. She knew she was old-fashioned, but she didn't like to think of her pretty daughter sharing with a man. And she didn't dare think what Derek would say. 'Is he married? A family who are letting out their spare room, perhaps?'

'No, Mum, he's not married.' Now Lara sounded irritated. 'It'll be fine. It won't be for long. Lots of girls share with men these days.'

'Yes, of course,' said Elizabeth doubt-fully. 'Tell me more about the job, dear. Is it promotion? We always thought you'd be a Head of Department sometime soon.' They had thought that was going to happen at the school in Glasgow, but for some reason it hadn't.

'It's not Head of Department,' said Lara, with more emphasis than Elizabeth thought was called for. Clearly she had said the wrong thing, again. 'It's Senior Geography Teacher, so it is a small promotion, but that's not why I went for it. I just want a change.'

'I'm sure you'll be very happy,' said Elizabeth encouragingly. 'Why don't we phone you back this evening and you can tell your father about it yourself?'

'No, no. You tell him. I'd better go now. Goodbye.'

Elizabeth put the phone down with a sigh. She wished she could do something to improve her relationship with her only child. She didn't know exactly when things had started to go wrong, but suddenly she was determined to try and put them right. She wasn't quite sure how. Perhaps not telling Derek that Lara was to be sharing with a man would be a good first step.

Spurred on by her mother's disapproval, Lara decided to go and look over Mick Jensen's house. She still had her doubts about sharing with him, but if the house was acceptable, she should probably take the room. He definitely wasn't her ideal housemate but the room was cheap and available. It would save so much time if she could stay there for the first few months.

On this second occasion, Lara drove down to Loreburn in her car. It had been in the garage the previous week, a place where it spent a good deal of time. She enjoyed the drive. She let the engine open up for an hour or so down the motorway, and then turning off over the Dalveen pass and came down through the winding roads she remembered from visits to Alex's gran.

The trees were gaunt and bare, but the sun was out, glinting off the occasional quaint red-sandstone house. It lifted her spirits to drive with fields and hills as far as the eye could see. Even the car seemed to like it, and didn't cough and splutter once. Maybe what they both needed was longer runs and a little fresh air.

The instructions Mick Jensen had given her proved to be surprisingly easy to follow, and ten minutes before the appointed time she drew up outside a semi-detached house identical to twenty or thirty others in the little estate. It was on the very edge of town, and you could see hills rising in those soft, hazy rolls into the distance.

She wondered if she should sit in the car and wait the extra ten minutes. Some people didn't like you to be early. But waiting was making Lara nervous, giving her too much time to think over what she might be letting herself in for. She climbed out of the car and strode up the short, slightly unkempt driveway and knocked on the glass front door.

It took Mick a minute or two to answer. He was wearing a torn T-shirt and a pair of tracksuit bottoms and had a bowl of cereal in one hand. He looked only half awake.

Lara smiled brightly. 'Sorry, I'm a little early. It didn't take me as long to get here as I expected.'

'Oh, it's you.' He squinted at her, the green eyes having difficulty staying open. 'Gosh, was it today you said you'd come?'

'It was.' She was beginning to feel annoyed with him again.

'Aye, well, you'd better come in then.' He stood back. 'It's not exactly tidy. I'd forgotten it was today you were coming and . . . ' He gave her a sudden grin. 'To tell you the truth, it probably wouldn't have made much difference if I'd remembered. But we have had a lady coming in weekly to do a basic clean, so it's not as bad as it might be.'

As Lara looked around she saw this was true. The décor might be early eighties and rather battered, and there was certainly far too much sports kit lying about, but there seemed to be an underlying cleanliness. Which was a relief. She knew the others teased her about it, but if you were born fastidious you had to accept it.

'Come into the kitchen, I'll get you a drink.' He finished his cereal and put the bowl in the sink. She stood just inside the doorway as he put on the kettle. It felt awkward. She hardly knew this man, how could she be considering sharing a house with him?

'Look, it's not luxurious or anything,' said Mick. He gestured around. 'Pretty basic, really, but we've got the essentials. Fridge, microwave.' He shot her another grin. He was waking up. 'There's even a cooker if you want to do proper meals. And I'll try and wash up a bit more often, but give me a kick if I forget. Steve, who I've been sharing with, was a bit untidy, and it doesn't kind of encourage you to clear up after yourself.'

'I suppose not.'

'Tea or coffee? What time did you get up this morning? Isn't it a two hour drive down here? I'm impressed. Rule number one; don't get up before nine at the weekend.'

'It's half-past ten.'

'I said not before nine. No limit to how late you can sleep, is there? I was helping Steve move into his new place yesterday, had a beer, you know how it is. No idea what time I got in but it was definitely late.'

'I hope you didn't drive.' Lara knew she sounded prim, but the conversation was making her feel breathless.

'Drive? No, I jogged back. It's only a couple of miles and it's good to clear the head, you know?'

Lara shook her own head slowly. Sharing with this man was going to be an education. Or maybe she would just try and steer clear of him. It was making her feel exhausted just listening.

She took the mug of coffee and said, 'Perhaps you could show me around. I've made an appointment to look at a couple of houses so I can't stay long.' She smiled to herself as she spoke. She had, indeed, arranged to see a couple of small, sensible houses. But also she hadn't been able to resist arranging to view Ladybank Row.

Mick led the way upstairs. 'Right, that's my room. I get the biggest one 'cos it's my house and I'm the messiest. This would be yours. It looks out the front so you've a view of the countryside, of sorts. Built in cupboard, double bed. Any other furniture you'd need to provide yourself. The bathroom's over there. Any questions?'

Lara took a while before she answered. She needed to slow this down. The curtains of 'her' room were an indeterminate pink/brown and the carpet was sand coloured. There was nothing you could take offence to, but nothing really to like either. 'It'll do fine,' she said firmly. After all, she wouldn't be staying here long. 'If you're still sure you want me as a tenant?'

'It sounds good to me.' He gave her another of those looks that she was almost sure he did on purpose, to discompose her. 'When can you move in?'

Lara tried to concentrate on practicalities. She said briskly, 'If it's OK with you, I'll pay a deposit now. I've brought some bags and boxes down with me and it'd be handy if I could leave them here.' She smiled doubtfully, hoping Mick wouldn't think her presumptuous. 'I'll sort more things out during the half-term holiday and move in the weekend before I start work. How would that be?'

'No problem. And you don't need to worry about a deposit, we can sort money out when you move in.'

'I'd rather do it this way. I'll pay you two weeks in advance, and then weekly thereafter. OK? How did you work it with your last tenant?'

'Er, not sure. He sort of paid when he remembered.'

Lara sighed. It felt a little too much like being back in a classroom of teenagers. She said repressively, 'That might be fine between friends, but ours is a business arrangement. And one other thing, is it OK with you if I have a friend to stay?'

For the first time since her arrival the good humour faded momentarily. 'A friend? Oh, yes, of course.'

'She'd share my room, and it would just be for a night or two. She's thinking of moving to Loreburn herself.' At least, Lara hoped she was.

'Ah,' said Mick, his bright smile returning. 'Loreburn seems to be popular at the moment. She'll be very welcome. The more the merrier, as far as I'm concerned.'

'She's . . . ' began Lara, and then hesitated. It wasn't her position to tell strangers about Alex's problems. Especially as she wasn't sure what they were herself. 'We'll keep out of your way. I'm very grateful to you for letting me stay.' She turned to face him and held out her hand. 'Shall we shake on it?'

She knew even as she did so that the gesture was a mistake. His hand closed around hers, warm and strong, and she felt as though he was pulling her in. Perhaps he felt the connection too, for he didn't let go immediately, but looked into her eyes, at almost the same level as his own, questioning.

'I'll go and get those bags,' she said.

Lara Has an Ambitious Idea

Lara knew persuading Alex to join her in her new life in Loreburn wasn't going to be easy. Alex was a staff nurse in one of the big Glasgow hospitals and for a while Lara had thought she was happy there. But since the beloved grandmother who had brought her up had died a year ago, Alex had withdrawn into herself. Always a quiet girl, her conversations were now almost monosyllabic. It was becoming difficult to persuade her to venture out except to go to work. Things had to change.

She didn't tell Alex all her plans at once. The first thing was to get her to visit Loreburn, something she hadn't done since her grandmother's funeral.

'I don't want to go back there,' Alex had whispered.

'But you were happy there.' Lara was worried. Alex had never mourned her grandmother as she should have. She had merely shut down.

Maybe if she could persuade her friend to take the step of revisiting what had once been her home, then she could move on. And thinking about Alex gave Lara something positive to do, and not dwell on her relationship with her own parents. Recent telephone conversations had been more difficult than usual. It hurt that their only interest in her new life had been disappointment she hadn't got promotion and horror she would be sharing with a man.

'It'll be great,' she said encouragingly to Alex.

'Mmm,' was all the answer her friend vouchsafed, but she had, reluctantly, agreed to accompany her for a visit.

Lara hoped she was doing the right thing. The closer they came to Loreburn, the more tense Alex became. Lara negotiated the last bend of the Dalveen pass and they began to drop down towards Loreburn. Alex sat beside her, clutching her ugly, bulky handbag with both hands. Lara bit her lip. She really, really hoped this was going to work.

'Aren't we going to your new house?' said Alex, when Lara parked the car outside a busy garden centre where she planned to have lunch. The place was new so could hold no memories for Alex.

'We'll eat here, my treat,' she said encouragingly. It was a good move. Alex began to relax a little. Food was her refuge. Well, that was all right for now.

When they had finished their main course, Alex looked longingly at the counter of freshly baked cakes, but Lara had other plans.

She had been so pleased with herself when she first had this marvellous idea. Now the time had come to share it and she wasn't so sure. 'Let's get on, we have a busy afternoon ahead. We'll save the coffee and cakes for a reward, later.'

She took Alex's shrug as agreement and stood up with more determination than she felt. Perhaps this was a mistake. Getting Alex down to Loreburn had been a success of sorts and she didn't want to push her too hard. But she needed to act quickly, if she was going to get the property she had in mind. At first it had been just a daydream, but the more she had thought it over the more it had seemed to make sense. The only problem had been whether Alex would agree.

Anyway, there was no chance of backing out of the viewing. She had agreed to collect the key from the solicitor and Lara always kept to arrangements once made. She sighed, sure now this wasn't going to work. She was clearly quite mad, but at least it might give her friend something to laugh about. If Alex ever started laughing again.

When she parked the car at the roadside before the line of boarded-up terraced houses which constituted Ladybank Row, she couldn't help smiling. She had really tried to be sensible and had viewed other smaller, more modern properties. That was the sort of thing everyone would expect of her, including herself, but her heart hadn't been in them. So she had given in and visited the properties again, and fallen in love.

The little terraced row was just as she remembered. Apparently, the houses had been built in the 1930s. They were partly pebble-dashed and partly red sandstone, with roofs of slate, which gave a solidity to the place you didn't get with something more modern, like Mick's semi. The architect had introduced a whimsical variety of roof heights and slopes and a seemingly haphazard arrangement of windows. Lara could easily ignore the overgrown gardens and blocked-off doorways. She could see what it might become.

'You've brought me to see this?' said Alex. She didn't sound impressed.

Lara said encouragingly, 'They're good solid houses. And they're going cheap.'

'They're ex-council houses,' said Alex gloomily. 'Aren't they?'

'Are they?' said Lara. Having been brought up in the various ex-pat communities of the world, she had never got the hang of identifying things like council housing. 'Does it matter?'

Alex shrugged and looked around at the rusting metal fence that hid the industrial estate, and the overgrown trees at the back where the railway line ran. She swung her arms about to keep her warm, and pulled a face. 'Which one are you interested in?'

'They're all for sale,' said Lara casually. 'But I've got the key to the end one. Let's have a look at that.'

The front door was held shut by a heavy padlock. It didn't look welcoming, but you could see why it was there. Marks where a crow bar had been used on the door jam were clearly in evidence.

Once inside, the rooms were dark. What else could you expect, when the windows were boarded up? And even Lara had to admit that it smelt damp. 'The rooms are nice and big, aren't they?' she said brightly. 'Two good-sized rooms down here, plus the kitchen. Come upstairs, you can see better up there.'

'No lights,' said Alex, flicking a switch on and off.

'The electricity's been disconnected, of course.'

Lara marched upstairs, and Alex followed more slowly. It was better up here. There was a charming little window on the landing, two large, bright bedrooms, a bathroom and separate toilet.

'Not bad is it?'

Alex shrugged.

'It could be made really nice. And they're selling the houses for peanuts.'

Alex went over to the bedroom window and stared out at the wilderness below. Like the house itself, the size of the garden was generous, but its neglect was complete. 'It looks like it's been empty ages.'

'The whole row has been on the market about six months, but some of the houses haven't been lived in for longer than that.'

They stayed in the largest bedroom, Alex still at the window. Lara admired the pleasant proportions of the room and almost managed to ignore the mottled purple walls.

She took a deep breath and said, 'Shall I tell you how much it's on the market for?'

'If you want.'

Lara named an amount that was slightly more than the value of her flat in Glasgow and Alex was sufficiently roused to say, 'They're mad. They'll never get that for a house in this state. I thought you said it was cheap!'

Lara hesitated, trying to keep her face straight. This was the really good part. 'That's not for one house. It's for the whole row.'

Alex stared at her. 'The whole row . . . ?'

'Yep. The whole lot. Now, that's what I call a bargain.' Lara gave a little twirl. Normally she wasn't given to demonstrations of emotion but she couldn't keep the excitement in. 'Don't you think that's amazing? It's an absolute bargain. I just knew, when I first walked past and saw all those quaint little windows and the funny pointy roofs, this was a special place. And when I saw the price, well . . . '

Alex frowned. 'But why would you want to buy the whole row? How many are there? Four? Five? You'd struggle to do up one.'

'There are four of them. All fairly similar in size and layout except the one at the far end, which has three bedrooms.'

Alex shook her head, as if struggling to take all this in. Lara supposed it was quite a shock. The idea had come to her gradually, so she'd had time to get used to it.

'Are you serious?'

'Absolutely.' Lara grinned. The cold feet she had had about sharing her idea were now a distant memory. The possibilities were bubbling up inside her. Life in Loreburn was going to be good, she just had to persuade Alex of this. 'I'm very serious. This is a once in a lifetime opportunity.'

'But Lara, you've got a full-time teaching job. What you're talking about here — this is property development.' For once Alex had been shocked out of her lethargy, which was just what Lara had intended.

'It's only on a very small scale,' said Lara, wheedling. 'One of the houses would be for me. Two could be done up to be sold. And I thought the last one, well, I thought you might like that.'

'Me?' said Alex.

'Yes. Don't you see how brilliant it is? I could practically buy the whole lot straight out myself, but then I wouldn't have a penny to do them up. You're not happy in your job in Glasgow, you know you're not. You need a project and you've always been brilliant at making houses look good, not to mention gardens. Look on it as a project.'

Lara was pleased to see she had her

friend's full attention now. 'I think you're crazy.'

'No. I'm not. You keep saying you don't know what to do with the money your gran left you. Well, this is ideal. She would be so pleased to think you had come back to live in Loreburn.'

'I don't want to come back and live in Loreburn.'

'You don't have to stay for ever,' said Lara quickly, worried she was moving too fast. 'You could look on this as taking a year out. Then you could go back to nursing, or travel, or whatever . . . '

'But . . . '

'It'd be brilliant. I really need you to do this with me, Lexi.'

'I don't know if I can.' Alex shook her head doubtfully, her long plait swinging. It was the most animation Lara had seen from her in months. 'Repainting a couple of rooms is one thing, but doing up a whole house. A whole row of houses . . . '

'We could think about it, at least,' Lara

said hopefully. 'What do you say? Alex?'

'I don't know. I really don't know.'

Lara crossed her fingers, willing this to be a good sign, and moved on. 'We need to move fairly quickly if we're going to make an offer. The houses were over-priced initially. The solicitor told me that. Since they dropped the price at the beginning of this month they're starting to get some interest. We wouldn't want to lose out on them, would we?'

'This is all so sudden,' said Alex, still perplexed.

Lara gave her a hug. 'I know, but it's a good kind of sudden. Isn't it? What do you say, Alex?'

'I'll think about it,' said Alex. Then she almost smiled, her pale plump face lightening. 'You know, it would be really nice not to have to do a late shift on Ward 22 ever again.'

'You won't regret it,' said Lara.

'I only said I'd think about it.'

'But you'll agree, just you wait and see.'

★ ★ ★

As far as Mick was concerned, life was getting better and better. He had liked the look of Lara Mason from the moment he saw her striding towards the school gates, slim and determined. And then she had agreed to take the room, and was going to introduce him to one of her female friends. He had had high hopes this Alex would be as attractive and interesting as Lara.

So when he met her, the only word for his reaction was disappointment. She was short and plump and somehow faded, withdrawn into herself. It was hard to imagine her having anything to do with smart and snappy Lara. She didn't meet his eyes when they were introduced and her feet dragged as Lara chivvied her up the stairs.

When Lara came down, alone, a few minutes later, he found himself at a loss for what to say.

'Alex is having a bath. Hope that's OK? You're not short of hot water are you?'

'No, no problem.'

'That's good. Alex's had a bit of a hard time recently, so I've put in loads of bubble bath and stuff that's supposed to help you relax. I hope she'll take the chance to wind down.'

He realised that she was trying to apologise for her friend. 'No problem,' he said again, feeling ashamed. 'And it's good to see you here at last. Now you just need to unpack all your things.'

'Yes.' Lara pulled a face, wrinkling the small, straight nose. 'I didn't realise I had so much.'

'Put some of the boxes in the spare room, if you like. It's hard to unpack when everything is on top of you.'

'But that's your study, isn't it?'

The room contained a desk with computer, an exercise bike, and an awful lot of rubbish. 'That's the theory, but . . . A few more boxes won't make any difference.'

'Thanks,' she smiled at him and he was pleased he had made the offer. Perhaps he could find a way to do her some more favours. Lara continued, 'I've got some food in the car, we did some shopping before we came home. Is it OK if I bring it in?'

'Absolutely. Plenty of space.' Mick opened a cupboard to demonstrate, realised that it contained one rusting baking tray and an awful lot of dust, and closed it quickly. 'I'll, er, give this a wipe out whilst you bring things in.'

He had seen her lip begin to curl at the state of his kitchen, but she bit back any comment and nodded. 'That's kind of you. Thanks.'

He watched as she turned to leave.

When he saw the array of specialist pastas, the breads and salads and bottles of wine she had brought, he was more determined than ever to hang around. Life was looking good.

Someone Takes an Interest in Lara

Lara was a little nervous on her first day at work. She had been into school the previous week to talk over some details with her new Head of Department, and the man had seemed pleasant enough. But Lara couldn't help thinking of Miss Dunlop, her Head of Department in Glasgow. She had been charming until she was actually in post. And then . . . Well, best not to think of that now.

Alex had actually hugged her before she took the train north and said she would return soon. Everything was going well. No reason at all why it shouldn't continue that way.

Her first class was a group of First Years, so small and sweet that she almost unbent and smiled at them. She remembered just in time her experiences as a probationary teacher when she had been too friendly too soon. She had never got the discipline back, so she kept this class on a tight rein. They worked hard and possibly even learnt something by the end of the lesson.

The period after break she had Fourth Years for Modern Studies. She kept to her no-nonsense approach, questioning them on work done to date and then setting them a rather stiff revision worksheet. She had to be particularly tough with this sort of group or they'd walk all over her.

And so the day passed, not too badly on the whole. The staff seemed friendly. There were one or two smiles when they learned she was sharing the house with Mick Jensen, which made Lara uncomfortable, so she ignored them. Everyone would soon realise that the two of them were nothing more than acquaintances. The fact they were both single, and Mick was so good-looking, shouldn't matter at all.

The house was empty when she got home and she decided to use the time to do a little cleaning in the kitchen. It was the sort of thing she enjoyed doing and it left her free to think at the same time.

Mick was an enigma to her. He seemed so easy-going, yet she had learnt enough in one day's teaching to know the school children idolised him. And, despite their teasing, the other staff seemed to respect him.

'What on earth are you doing?' demanded a voice behind her, making Lara jump. Mick had a really annoying habit of catching her unawares.

She hoped she wasn't blushing. It felt strange having him in the room with her when he had been so much in her thoughts.

She sat back on her heels. 'Cleaning. What does it look like?'

'Ah,' said Mick doubtfully. 'Isn't it clean enough?'

Lara sighed. He had made a show of wiping down the cupboards the other day, but he must realise he hadn't done a proper job, surely? Even if she wasn't going to stay here long, one glance at the cupboards had made her realise she couldn't put up with them like this.

'I could do that,' said Mick, looking at the bleach and disinfectant and scourers she had lined up. 'Probably.' His expression was a mixture of horror and bemusement.

'I've almost finished. Everything will keep fresh much longer once I've done this.'

'It will?'

'Absolutely.'

He made a pot of tea, treading warily around her, but seeming in no hurry to leave. He leant back in one of the chairs and settled down to watch her work. 'You're really good at this, aren't you?' he said.

'It's not exactly rocket science, cleaning a kitchen.'

'Ah.' After a pause he said, 'I never thought to ask Debbie, who cleans for us, to do the cupboards.'

'So I see.'

'How did you enjoy your first day?'

he asked, as though suddenly remembering that he should.

'It was OK.'

'That good?'

'I'm just finding my feet,' said Lara cautiously. She didn't want him to know how nervous she had been.

'The kids are scared of you,' he said, head on one side. 'I'm impressed. How did you manage that?'

She was surprised. 'I'm sure they're not scared of me. I hope they'll respect me. That way I can get them to do the best work possible. That's my job, isn't it?' She felt uncomfortable at the thought of people discussing her.

'Looks like old McIntyre chose well this time,' he said with a grin. 'I hope the rest of the staff are making you welcome?'

'They seem nice,' she said.

'They're not a bad bunch. I'll introduce you to some more tomorrow. There's no football practice at lunch time, for once. I could show you the canteen, if you want.'

'Thanks. That's very kind.' Lara hadn't expected him to make so much effort. 'I'm going to make myself an omelette and some salad for my supper,' she said, rising to her feet. 'Do you want to join me? You've probably got other plans, but you're more than welcome . . . '

The face he turned towards her showed more delight than she thought was called for. 'That sounds brilliant.'

Lara didn't know how she had got herself into that. She hadn't intended to get too friendly with this handsome, flippant man. And here she was offering to cook for him. Well, she couldn't back out now. But she would need to make sure he didn't start expecting this every day.

* * *

Elizabeth spread out the particulars of six or seven houses on the coffee table before her. She was excited. This was the day she and Derek had been waiting for for decades. They had kept a small flat in Cheshire for holidays, and to keep a foot on the property ladder. Now they were selling that and buying a house of their very own! A place to live for the rest of their lives. Elizabeth had had enough of beautiful rented accommodation. She couldn't wait to set to work on her own place.

Derek had been adamant they should look for somewhere in the south of England, because they were so used to the warmer weather. They had decided to look in Devon, and although the prices were high the properties, the scenery and the towns were all so beautiful Elizabeth was itching to get over there and start her new life.

Obviously they couldn't buy anything without seeing it first, so it had been decided she would fly over to the UK at the end of the week and view two or three properties they particularly liked. She was nervous at the idea of making a decision without Derek, but he couldn't get the time off work and he said he trusted her judgment when it came to houses. She was surprised. She hadn't thought he trusted her judgment about very much at all.

They had narrowed the lists down from hundreds to twenty or so, and now down to six. She thought she would go and see all of those, although her heart was already very drawn to a modern bungalow in a village not far from Exeter. It was just what they needed and the views were spectacular.

The only drawback was that it would be so far from Lara. She sighed. She wished again that Lara had told them she was thinking of changing her job, it would have been wonderful if she, too, had moved south. Maybe it wasn't too late to try and persuade her? She decided to phone and find out.

Elizabeth was a little disconcerted when a man answered the phone. He was polite, but he sounded so young, and she really wished Lara had gone for a more usual sharing arrangement.

'Mum?' said Lara when she eventually came to the phone. 'Is everything all right? You don't usually phone at this time.'

'Yes, everything is fine. A mother can phone her daughter when she feels like it, can't she?'

'Er, yes. Of course. As long as it's not the middle of the night.'

Elizabeth bit her lip. Once again, their conversation had got off to a bad start. 'I was wondering how your first week at school had gone,' she said.

'It was all right,' said Lara, guarded as ever.

'I'm sure it'll take you a while to settle in, and then it will be lovely,' said Elizabeth encouragingly.

'Yes,' said Lara politely. 'And how are you and Dad?'

'We're both fine. Actually, Lara . . . ' Elizabeth hesitated. Perhaps she should have given her daughter more warning. 'Actually, I'm coming over to England next week.'

'Next week?' Lara sounded more

amazed than pleased.

'Yes. You know your father retires at the end of June and we're thinking of buying a house to retire to? I'm coming over to have a look at one or two.'

'Is Dad really retiring?'

'Yes, dear. He is sixty-five in May.'

'I know. But I just thought . . . Work is his life, isn't it?'

'He has enjoyed his work and been very successful at it. But now we're both looking forward to returning to the UK.'

'Oh,' said Lara. Elizabeth wished she had discussed this with her daughter sooner. Somehow, it had never cropped up. 'That's nice.'

'Yes. I'll be flying in to London a week on Monday. I wondered if you might be able to pop down and meet me?'

'I'm not sure. I'm working, as you know. Why aren't you flying in to Manchester? I presume that's where you'll be looking for houses?'

'Well, no,' said Elizabeth. 'We've

decided on Devon. Your father has always loved the south west and the winters are so much milder there . . . '

'Devon?' said Lara blankly. 'But that's miles away.'

'But it's very lovely. I hoped you might look around with me, see what you thought. I don't suppose you would consider moving to the south west yourself . . . '

'Mum, I've just moved here! I've just started a new job! I have moved to the south west, it's just that I've moved to the south west of Scotland, not England. I thought it wouldn't be too far from you if you came back to Cheshire, but Devon!' Lara sounded quite put out.

'Couldn't you come and spend a few days with me down there, see what you think?'

'No, Mum, I couldn't. It's term-time, remember.'

'But you haven't bought anything there, yet, have you? I thought if you really liked the area around Exeter you might be tempted . . . ' Elizabeth's voice tailed off. It had been a long shot.

'I'm buying a property up here,' said Lara abruptly. 'Alex and I have already put in an offer.'

'Goodness, so quickly? I thought you'd need a bit of time to look around. But I suppose if you've seen the ideal place and can just move in, then that's that.

'Yes. She's thinking of moving down to Loreburn too.'

'That's nice.' Elizabeth waited for her daughter to say more, but she didn't. Lara had always been very good at not giving out information, as though she thought her parents weren't interested, or, worse, might disapprove. That wasn't the case at all.

'Do you think you could manage a quick trip down south to see me? Maybe for the weekend? It would be lovely.'

'To Devon? No. There's no way I could get there and back in a weekend. Why don't you come up here?'

'I'm afraid I can't. The ticket your dad has booked for me is just for seven days.'

'Never mind,' said Lara.

Elizabeth realised she didn't know if her daughter was hurt or relieved. Another conversation had passed and they were further apart than ever.

★ ★ ★

On a Friday evening Mick made his way to the less-than-perfect football fields on the rougher side of town. He knew he'd said to Steve that he wasn't going to waste his time here any longer, but something drew him back. It wasn't the part of town that he'd come from, but there was something so familiar about it.

The poorly cut grass, the scruffy bad-mouthed kids. And the desire to do something, and do it well.

It was already nearly seven in the evening and dark except for the half-hearted floodlights. The boys were standing around, smoking surreptitiously, occasionally kicking a ball.

'Hey, where're the teams?'

One youth kicked the ball towards Mick. 'You weren't here, were you? Who's gonna organise it if you're not here?' Ryan had attended Loreburn High until the previous summer, but he had now left the education system for boredom or worse.

Mick bent to pick up the ball. 'It didn't help that I was here, last week.'

'That was just those stupid Townhouse kids.'

'Two sides to the fighting, as far as I could see.'

'We didn't start it,' said Ryan, his lower lip protruding.

'OK, OK, let's forget last week. Who's up for a game tonight?'

With a careful lack of enthusiasm, the youths scuffed their feet but gathered round. Ten minutes later there were enough of them for four teams of seven-a-side and the games started. Mick was relieved. He hadn't been sure how it would go tonight, after the trouble last week. It might have scared off some of the youths and encouraged others to come back for more of the same. Instead, it seemed to have shocked them into something like good behaviour.

They actually managed a mini-tournament without serious flare-ups. As Mick headed to meet Steve for a drink afterwards, he was quietly pleased. These kids needed something. Not that a couple of hours a week of football was ever going to solve their problems. He sighed.

When a car pulled up beside him he was surprised to see the occupant. Ed McAnulty, Steve's older brother, didn't normally make time to talk to Mick these days.

'I hear you've got a new housemate,' said Ed without preamble. He was a large man with very dark hair and eyes. He had never been prone to small talk so Mick didn't take offence at the curt tone.

'Yes, Steve eventually got round to buying a place of his own.'

Ed scowled. 'I would have helped him out if he'd asked me.'

Mick shrugged and said nothing. He had always hated being caught in the arguments between these two.

'Your housemate's a teacher from Glasgow, isn't she? I presume she's looking to buy property herself. Any idea what she's looking at?'

'No,' said Mick, puzzled now. Ed was a builder, having taken over his father's small business on his death and expanded it steadily since. Steve's refusal to join him in the business was the main bone of contention between the two. As far as Mick knew, Ed wasn't at the stage of building complete houses, so he couldn't see what Lara's plans might have to do with him.

'She's not looking to take on something run down and do it up?' asked Ed.

'Not as far as I know.' Mick had avoided discussing possible houses with

Lara. He hoped that way she might end up staying longer at his place.

'I just wondered,' said Ed, and began to wind up his window. 'I'll see you around.'

Mick shook his head as the van pulled away. Now what had that been about?

It's Always Been a Bit of a Dump

Lara hadn't been telling the absolute truth when she said to her mother she and Alex had already put in an offer for Ladybank Row. But with a bit of luck they would do so very soon.

Since their visit to the properties, Lara had arranged for a survey to be done and had sent the results to her friend in Glasgow, hoping this would spur her on to make a decision. It seemed that Alex was slowly moving towards agreement, but it was taking too long for Lara's liking. If they didn't make an offer soon they might lose the properties.

'Alex, I thought you'd be really keen,' she said encouragingly, on one of their frequent telephone conversations. 'The solicitor says we need to put in an offer on Monday if we want to go ahead. Come on, just tell me straight. Do you want to be part of this?'

Alex gave a nervous laugh. 'You want it straight?'

Lara bit her lip and said on a sigh, 'Yes.'

'OK, here it is then.' Alex paused. 'I've decided to give in my notice. I've informed the bank that I'll be withdrawing some of my money in thirty days' time. I think we should definitely go ahead.'

Lara sat down suddenly on the stairs in Mick's hallway. 'You do?'

'Ye-es.' Alex still sounded cautious. 'We can give this a try, can't we?'

'Yes. Yes, we can. And succeed. So can I put in an offer on Monday?'

Alex gave only a small moan of protest. 'Do we have to do it so soon?'

'If we don't want to risk losing the house we do.'

'OK then . . . Go ahead.'

At the end of the phone call Lara stayed seated on the stairs for a few minutes, hugging herself with excitement.

'Are you OK?' said Mick, when he

swung open the front door and found her still sitting there.

'Yes. Fine. Brilliant, in fact.' Lara beamed at him.

'That's good.' He let the small rucksack fall from his back and raised an eyebrow, questioningly.

Lara rose to her feet. Her legs now felt strong enough to hold her. 'I've been trying to persuade my friend, Alex, to join me in a . . . a kind of plan I've got. And she just said yes. I'll tell you about it if you want. And I'm going to have a glass of wine and celebrate surviving my second week at a new school.'

'Now that's what I call a good idea. I need a shower but I won't be five minutes. Pour me a glass.'

She realised that he had once again run back from school. How could anyone do so much exercise from choice? And find it so easy? He gave her a grin as he headed up the stairs past her and she wondered again if it was a mistake to get too friendly with him. For the last week or so she had managed to forget that he was a man and concentrate on what a pleasant companion he could be.

Now he was making her nervous again. Perhaps it was just because this was the first time she had had a male housemate. She had to be careful not to be silly about it.

She opened a bottle of white wine and sat down at the little kitchen table to study the Ladybank Row particulars for the umpteenth time. Since Alex's visit she had driven past the Row every single day. She couldn't remember when last she had been so enthusiastic about anything outside her work.

And work wasn't going too badly, either. She was a little disappointed to find that Mr McIntyre had been absolutely honest in his assessment of her predecessor. All classes were way behind in the curriculum. But it wasn't as if she was new to this. She'd been teaching for over six years now and with a bit of hard work she would have them up to speed by the end of the summer term.

She had responded cautiously to one or two friendly overtures from other members of staff and had been pleased when a group of older women had invited her along to the cinema. Nothing like this would have happened at her last school, especially not after the arrival of Miss Dunlop.

She had settled into an easy routine with Mick. Despite his scruffy clothes and casual demeanour, he seemed to be a genuinely nice man.

'Penny for them,' said Mick. She hadn't heard him come down stairs and now he was standing right beside her, hair wet, smelling of clean clothes and a kind of minty shower gel.

'What? Oh, er, nothing. Here, have a glass.' She picked up the open bottle and poured one quickly, disconcerted that she had once again been thinking of him at the very moment he appeared. She pushed the glass to the other side of the table so that he had to go and sit down, leaving her some space. Was it her imagination, or had he been standing too close?

He raised his glass to her. 'Here's to a successful first fortnight. And many more.'

'Thanks. It's not been too bad. Let's hope it continues that way.'

'They like you. You'll be fine.'

'Who do?'

'The teachers think you're competent, so they're relieved. But the kids think you're cool, and that's what really counts.'

'They do not,' said Lara, hoping she wasn't blushing. 'I hope. The last thing I need is for the kids to like me. I thought you said they were scared of me.'

'Wary, rather than scared. I was only joking about that the other day, you did realise, didn't you? And it doesn't do you any harm that they think you're so pretty.' He watched her face for a reaction and laughed when she blushed.

'Ha,' she said awkwardly. She knew this, at least, was a joke. She had been a skinny scarecrow with too-big eyes ever since she could remember.

'It's true. They think you're a vast improvement on poor Mr Hartman.'

'Who by all accounts was way past his best. Thanks for the compliment.' She was much more at ease with this kind of comment.

'Don't pity him. He was delighted to retire on the grounds of ill health, lucky thing.'

'You're going to have to work harder at being unhealthy yourself, if that's your ambition.'

'I have one or two bad habits,' he said happily, rummaging in one of the cupboards for a giant bag of crisps. 'Help yourself.'

Lara reached across for a handful. She hadn't even thought about what she would eat that night. It had been a relief to get to Friday, and then the message from the solicitor had put everything else out of her mind.

'You were going to tell me about your plan,' he said, settling back in his chair. 'Is there some secret reason for your move to Loreburn?'

Lara was more than happy to enthuse about the four houses that comprised Ladybank Row. She wasn't normally so talkative, but when it came to Ladybank Row she couldn't help herself. It was going to be so good. 'And now Alex has finally agreed she's willing to join me. Isn't it brilliant?' She waited for Mick to be impressed.

Instead he frowned and said, 'You're not serious, surely? I know the place you mean. Down that little alley by the railway station? It's always been a bit of a dump.'

'It's got a lot of potential,' said Lara, put out.

'I have to admit I haven't been round there recently. If I'd given it any thought I'd have said they were going to demolish them.'

'I understand they had to move the tenants as the houses no longer comply with current health and safety laws. That's why they're being sold off so cheaply.'

'That's why they're probably only fit to be pulled down. It'll cost a fortune to put them right. And you two girls are taking on something like that?'

Now Lara was offended. 'We're two capable people taking on a challenging but achievable project.'

'Huh. What do you know about the property market?'

'A little.'

'About building work?'

'Not a lot.'

'Then either you've got money to burn, or you're mad. Or both.'

'Thanks for the vote of confidence. What was that about me being competent?' Lara was more hurt than she would have expected.

'As a teacher. This is something else. This is the sort of thing Steve's brother, Ed McAnulty, might get into. He's got his own building firm. Whatever gave you the idea?'

'I . . . ' said Lara, beginning in the same heated vein and then tailing off. 'I don't really know. But I still think it's a good idea.' She was riled and worried by his doubts in a way she hadn't been when persuading Alex to go in with her. 'What do you know about it, anyway?'

He shrugged and spread out his hands. 'Absolutely nothing. Which is why I bought a place like this and haven't lifted a finger since I moved in.'

'I noticed.'

'Well, if you want to practice your DIY skills . . . '

'We're not necessarily going to do the building work ourselves. We'll pay others to do that.'

'Money to burn.' His hair was drying, blond and messy, and he ran his fingers through it and shook his head, sadly.

Lara could feel fear and irritation rise within her. What if he was right? 'I don't think so,' she said, trying to sound sure. 'And neither does Alex.' She hoped. Was Alex just looking for a reason to leave Glasgow and her awful job? She took a sip of wine. Suddenly all the pleasure had gone out of the day.

Lara Feels Threatened

Lara was alone in the house on the Monday evening when there was a hammering on the door. She had been looking forward to a quiet few hours of marking and was not pleased to be disturbed.

She made her way into the hall and hesitated, looking at the large shape she could see through the frosted glass. Mick was out and she wasn't expecting any visitors. She was glad she had locked the door, but now realised that there was neither a spy hole nor a safety chain.

'Ye-es?' she shouted. 'Who is it?'

'It's Ed. Open the door.'

'Er, Mick's not here.'

'I don't care whether Mick's there or not. Let me in.'

'Who are you looking for?'

'Lara. Are you Lara?'

'Ye-es,' she said doubtfully.

'You're the one I want to speak to.' The man's tone moderated slightly. 'Look, can I come in?'

Lara was beginning to feel silly, shouting the conversation through the door. Loreburn was hardly a criminal hotspot. And the visitor seemed to know Mick. She opened the door slightly but kept her foot against it, as though that would stop the huge bear of a man. 'Who did you say you were?'

'Ed. Ed McAnulty.'

'Oh, Steve's brother.' She remembered Mick mentioning the man's name and was relieved, although she wasn't sure why that should make it all right. She opened the door a little more and he strode in without waiting for an invitation.

'So you know my brother, do you? I should have guessed.'

'Erm, how can I help you?' said Lara. Ed had checked the sitting room, as though not believing Mick was out, and now paced up and down the small kitchen.

'I want to know what you're playing at,' he said, coming to a halt at the sink and turning to face her. He had dark hair and was heavily built. His expression was grim.

Lara was starting to feel nervous again. 'I don't know what you mean.'

'Coming down here, thinking you can throw your weight around because we're a small town and you're from Glasgow.'

'I still don't know what you're talking about.'

'Of course you do. Was it my brother who put you up to it? I should never have mentioned the flaming houses to him.' The man's voice began to rise and his colour deepened. 'I knew it had to be an inside job when I heard someone had put in an offer before me. I was the only one interested, I knew I was, and then you turn up out of the blue.'

Realisation began to dawn on Lara. 'You're talking about Ladybank Row.'

Although what it had to do with him she still had no idea.

'I wonder how you guessed,' said the man sarcastically. 'Now, what's your game? How much have you offered? You're not really serious, are you? You're just trying to put a spoke in the works.'

'I don't choose to discuss this with you,' said Lara, bridling.

'Tell me what you offered. I'll find out, whether you tell me or not. You just want to cause me problems. Steve has put you up to this, hasn't he?'

'I really don't know what you're talking about,' said Lara. 'I've never even met your brother. You're being ridiculous.'

He ignored her protests. 'I can tell you now I'm not easy to manipulate. I want those houses and I'm going to get them. At a price I choose to pay. Are you listening?'

Lara stared at him, wishing frantically that Mick was here. He would know how to handle this. He had mentioned the man was a good builder. Why hadn't he warned her he was also a maniac? 'You're not making any sense,' she said.

'Don't think playing all innocent will wash with me. Nobody wanted those houses except me. I know that. I've waited long enough, bided my time. And then you appear out of the blue, only a couple of weeks after I mention them to Steve. Don't think I can't put two and two together.' He glowered across the kitchen at her, his huge bulk seeming to fill the space. 'I think you'll find it's a good idea to stop wasting my time and withdraw your offer.'

'I'd like you to leave,' said Lara, trying to sound confident. It wasn't so much the man's size that she found intimidating as his almost tangible fury.

'Tell me one thing first, has your offer been accepted yet?'

She hesitated. 'I'm not in a position to discuss that.'

'Which means it hasn't.' He moved towards her. 'Look, you know you're not serious about this. I suggest you withdraw it now. It'll be simpler all round.'

'We are serious,' said Lara, but her voice sounded feeble even to her. She shook her head. The man was so large and so very angry. She didn't deal well with head-on emotion like this. She just wanted him to leave. She walked to the front door, trying not to show she was shaking. 'I think you should go. Now.'

The man glared at her a moment longer and then shrugged. 'You haven't heard the last of me,' he said as he stalked out.

Lara closed and locked the door. What on earth had all that been about? She felt sick, as she used to do after a confrontation with awful Miss Dunlop. She had come to Loreburn to escape this kind of thing.

She couldn't believe they had done anything to provoke this outburst. As she stood there, the fear began to fade into anxiety. What if this man was right? What if he could make life difficult, snatch Ladybank Row away from them? She shuddered. Everything had been going so well. She should have known it couldn't continue.

* * *

For once Mick remembered to use his key when he arrived home. He was so occupied with congratulating himself on this he didn't immediately notice Lara standing in the doorway of the kitchen.

'You OK?' He off-loaded his duffle bag and the rucksack he used for his food shopping.

'What? Yes, I'm fine.'

'Have you had bad news?' He frowned at her. Normally she didn't have much colour in her cheeks, but now she was completely white.

She said slowly. 'I — we — had a visitor.'

Mick was worried. What visitor could make her look like that? 'Come and sit down,' he said. 'Tell me about it.'

He swept aside the pile of books she had set neatly out on the table and set about making a pot of tea. 'Now, who was it?'

'It was your friend, Steve's, brother. Ed.'

'Ed McAnulty? What on earth was he doing here?' Mick was more bemused than ever. How odd that Ed should crop up twice in a few days. Previously he hadn't seen him for months. He didn't have anything against Ed, it just hadn't seemed loyal to Steve to socialise with him. After their brief chat on Friday, the last thing he would have expected was a visit from the man. 'Did you phone him to talk about building work?'

'No, nothing like that. I might have phoned him if you'd given me his number, but I certainly won't now.' She shuddered.

'He knows Steve doesn't live here anymore,' said Mick. 'So why on earth did he call?'

Lara swallowed. 'Ladybank Row. I

think he's also after Ladybank Row.'

'And Ladybank Row is . . . ?'

'Those houses we want to buy, I told you about them. We put in an offer this morning and, somehow, he knew about it.'

'Ah,' said Mick. 'Oh dear.' It was starting to make a little too much sense. Ed must have had his eye on the properties. He wouldn't be at all pleased if someone else got in before him. Especially not a bunch of amateurs. Especially not a bunch of amateurs apparently connected to Steve.

'He seemed to think Steve was involved somehow. I really don't understand why.'

Mick sighed. 'I think I do.' All too well, he thought grimly. 'Was he unpleasant?'

'You could say.' Lara smiled faintly, the colour coming back to her cheeks.

'That's not on.' Mick suddenly felt very angry, but he didn't want to scare Lara more by showing it. He touched her hand. 'I know Ed has a bit of a temper but he's no right to take it out on you. Are you OK?'

She took a deep breath. 'I am now, thanks. I shouldn't have let it get to me so much.' She shook her head. 'For some reason he seemed to be more angry with Steve than anything. Maybe angry is an understatement.'

'They don't get on,' said Mick. 'Haven't ever done, really, but it's been even worse the last few years. Ed has this idea that Steve is trying to get one up on him, which isn't true. Steve's so easy going he couldn't be bothered to get one up on anyone, but you know what it's like with siblings.'

'I'm an only child,' said Lara. 'Maybe that's a good thing.'

'I have to say my sisters aren't too bad. I've always found them a bit of a soft touch, truth be told, but Ed and Steve have fought for as long as I can remember. It's strange. Ed's fine with everyone else.' He glanced at Lara who was looking disbelieving. 'Nearly everyone else.'

Lara gave a shudder and then picked up her mug, cupping her hands around it as though she was cold. 'He couldn't actually make us withdraw our offer, could he?'

'Of course not,' said Mick. He didn't add that Ed could always put in a higher one. He undoubtedly had the financial clout to do so.

Lara started to say something about getting back to her marking. Mick decided the best thing to do for the moment was to let her.

Lara and Mick Cross Swords

After a good night's sleep, Lara was able to put Ed McAnulty's visit into perspective. She had overreacted, as usual. It was just that she so hated a show of emotion like that. And the idea that Ladybank Row might be snatched from them when it was so nearly in their grasp was awful. She had got the impression from Mick the man had a fair amount of influence in the area, but surely he couldn't stop the Council considering their bid? And they had got in first.

She phoned Alex during her lunch break to discuss the situation with her.

'That was horrible for you,' said Alex, sounding worried. 'Are you all right?' Her concern made Lara pull herself together.

'Yes, I'm fine.'

'There isn't anything he can do, is

there?' said Alex. 'He can't stop them accepting our offer, can he?'

'Not unless he puts in a higher one.' Lara's heart sank at the thought. But she wasn't going to just sit back and let this happen. 'I'll get on to our solicitor straight away, see what he can find out.'

'That's a good idea,' said Alex. Lara was glad her friend wasn't using this as an excuse to back out. It seemed that she too was now really keen on Ladybank Row. She was showing more interest in this than she had in anything for months. All the more reason for making sure their bid was successful.

Lara arrived home that afternoon full of energy and wondered what to do. The solicitor was doing what he could for Ladybank Row, all her lessons were prepared for the next day. She supposed she could go for a run, as Mick would have done, but the idea didn't really appeal.

She decided to go and do some food shopping, and was then tempted by the home furnishings store next to the supermarket. A little look inside wouldn't hurt, would it? Mick's house was so dull. There was nothing wrong with it, the settees were fairly new, the curtains of reasonable quality. But everything was so bland. Before she knew it Lara had filled a trolley with plush velour throws in colours of jewels, and cushions that sparkled with silk and sequins.

It wasn't a waste of money, she told herself. She would take all these things with her when she moved out. And it would be nice to make the house a little more inviting whilst she stayed there.

It didn't take her long to vacuum and dust Mick's sitting room and then rearrange the rather limited furniture, spreading her beautiful new purchases around. The difference was amazing! The room looked homely, warmer, like a place you would want to spend time. Very pleased with herself, Lara went to put the kettle on for a well-earned cup of tea.

She didn't hear Mick come in over the sound of the kettle and the first she knew of his arrival was a loud exclamation. 'What on earth have you done to my house?' He stood in the hallway, looking into the living room and then at her in the kitchen. For the first time since Lara had known him, he didn't look pleased.

'I just bought a few things . . . '

'Take over, why don't you?' Mick's face was flushed. It might have been from jogging home, but Lara didn't think so. He was actually angry. The easy-going smile was replaced by narrowed lips and flashing eyes. 'Don't mind me. I only own the place.'

'I'm sorry,' said Lara, quailing before him. 'I thought it would make a nice change . . . '

'I suppose it wasn't good enough for you? As I said when you moved in, you can do what you want to your room, but I didn't expect you to take over the whole house.'

'You didn't mind when I stocked the kitchen.' Lara was confused. He'd encouraged her to bring in her pots and pans, bowls and knives. Somehow brightening up the sitting room had just seemed like an extension of that. To her. Obviously not to him.

'That was different,' he said. 'Oh never mind. I'm going to have a shower.' He turned and strode up the stairs, taking two at a time.

Lara was almost in tears. First the argument with Ed McAnulty, and now this. She crept into the sitting room and began to pile up the throws and cushions. She could use them in her bedroom. It would make it a bit more interesting. And if Mick was going to be so grumpy, she could see herself spending rather a lot of time up there.

* * *

Mick didn't know why he was so annoyed with Lara. He took an extra-long shower so that he could calm down, and when he did he was ashamed of his outburst. He supposed the house was a bit dull. He really hadn't spent much time and energy on it. There always seemed to be something more important, such as football, or teaching, or . . . football.

Why shouldn't she try to make it a bit more comfortable if she wanted to? Actually, when he thought about it, it had looked rather nice. It had just been such a shock. And he had felt criticised. She could make things lovely in such a short time, and he hadn't managed it in the two years he had been here.

When he went back downstairs the brightly coloured cushions and blankets had disappeared. The room was back to boring beige and brown. And Lara was nowhere to be seen, although her bedroom door was closed.

He knocked hesitantly. 'Er, Lara?'
'Yes?'
'Can I have a word?'
She opened the door cautiously. Her face was paler than ever, she might even have been crying. Mick felt terrible.
'I'm sorry,' she said quickly. 'I shouldn't have done it, specially not

without asking you. I won't do it again and if you want me to move out . . . '

'Stop, stop! Of course I don't want you to move out.' He took a deep breath. 'I was going to ask if you might change your mind and bring the things back down. It did, well, it did look a lot better with them there.'

'But you said . . . '

'I overreacted,' said Mick firmly. 'I'm sorry. Can we start again?' He took a deep breath. 'You had this idea of making a few changes to the sitting room and I think that's excellent. I don't know why I didn't think of it myself. Now, perhaps we could take it all down . . . ?'

'Are you sure?' said Lara. The faint colour was coming back into her face. 'I'm really sorry for being so presumptuous.'

'Let's both stop apologising, shall we? You can do whatever it was you did to the room to make it so different, and I'll cook us a meal. It'll have to be cheese and beans on toast because that's about my limit, but I can assure you I do a very good cheese and beans on toast.'

He waited, holding his breath. Would she take the olive branch he was offering?

'That sounds perfect,' she said, and smiled. Mick wanted to shout his relief, but contented himself with a smile in return.

★　★　★

Lara had been going to ask a favour of Mick, but after the disagreement over her attempts at redecorating his house she changed her mind. She had seen how little he used his 'office' and had wondered if he would mind Alex staying there. It would be ideal for the girls to be close together in Loreburn, and would have meant a little extra money for Mick. Now she didn't want to tread on his toes so would have to think of something else.

In the meantime, she concentrated

on worrying about whether or not they were actually going to get Ladybank Row. The Council seemed to be taking forever to make up their mind: would they accept Lara and Alex's offer, accept Ed's offer (if he had made one), or go to a closing date? The not knowing was really getting to her.

Then, when she checked her mobile for messages one lunchtime, she found instructions from the solicitor to phone him immediately. He had something to report.

She couldn't make a call as important as this in public so she decided to nip home and phone from there. She tried to slip out of the staffroom without being caught in conversation, but Mick appeared just as she reached the door.

'You're in a hurry,' he said. 'Where are you off to?'

'I'm just, er, popping back to the house. Anything I can get for you?'

He smiled. 'Brilliant. You couldn't give me a lift, could you? I forgot I needed kit for circuit training this evening and I won't have the chance to go back after school.'

'Of course,' said Lara. She could hardly refuse. 'Is it all right if we go straight away?'

Mick nodded and fell in to step beside her. He didn't ask why she was going home at lunchtime, something she had never done before. She drove quickly along the now familiar streets, wiping her hands surreptitiously on the dark green linen dress. He glanced across at her. 'You seem nervous.'

Lara sighed. He would know soon enough why she had wanted to go back to the house. 'I need to phone the solicitor.'

'Good news?'

'I won't know until I speak to him, will I?'

'Why didn't you just phone from school?'

'I want somewhere private,' she said, hoping he would take the hint. And he seemed to. When they reached the house he went straight to the kitchen, most unusually closing the door behind him.

The solicitor was a man in his early sixties, slow-speaking and pedantic.

'Good afternoon young lady,' he said. 'I've been expecting to hear from you.'

'Yes. I phoned as soon as I could. Do you have any news?'

'I do indeed.' He cleared his throat. 'Matters didn't go exactly as I had anticipated, but I should be used to that after all the years I've worked in this business.'

'Yes?' Lara wanted to scream at him.

'Yes indeed. I'd like to know what game McAnulty and Sons are playing at, but so far I can't put my finger on it.'

'We didn't get it,' said Lara on a whisper.

'Oh yes, young lady. Oh yes indeed, your bid has been accepted. What I can't understand is that after all this delay yours was actually the only bid.'

'Ye-es!' Lara gave a whoop of delight. They had done it! She only half listened to the rest of Mr Brownlee's comments. She didn't care, she didn't need the details now. She just needed to know that they had won.

'Ladybank Row is ours!' She flung open the kitchen door and launched herself into Mick's arms, swinging him round in more of a dance than a hug. 'We got it. They've accepted our offer, no quibbles, can you believe it? That is so brilliant.'

He beamed back at her, his scepticism about the purchase apparently forgotten. 'Well done.'

'We got it!' She couldn't keep the smile off her face. 'I can't believe it. I was so worried. I don't know what we would have done if it hadn't worked out.'

'You deserve it.' He seemed genuinely pleased for her. 'You've put in a lot of effort already.'

'Maybe we do deserve it, but I couldn't dare hope, I didn't believe . . . ' She finally stood still, her enthusiasm making her breathless, a grin spreading across her face.

'Congratulations.' He ruffled her hair, laughing at her.

'Oh.' She could feel herself blushing. 'Thanks. Right. I've got to phone Alex. They've even agreed to an early entry date.' She gave a little twirl, shot him a slightly more guarded smile, and slipped back into the hall.

She wished she hadn't hugged him like that. Now he would think she was interested in him and she really wasn't. He was the happy-go-lucky type, a man who flirted with everyone in his light-hearted way. He really wasn't her type. She just wished she didn't have to work so hard at reminding herself of that.

Alex was as pleased as Lara, in her quiet way. 'Now we can really start planning,' she said. 'Oh, Lara, I'm so pleased.'

Lara was delighted, not only that their bid had been successful, but that Alex was so happy.

Mick came downstairs, carrying one of his inevitable bags of sports kit. 'Are you ready to head back? Otherwise we might be late and Mr McIntyre wouldn't be at all impressed by that.'

'Goodness,' said Lara, looking with horror at her watch. She couldn't believe how quickly the time had passed. 'Come on, let's go.'

Once they were in the car Mick was silent, as though thinking something over. She hoped he wasn't regretting having rented a room to her. Even though she had now bought a property of her own, it would be months before it was ready to be lived in. Should she say something to him about that?

'You know I said I didn't use my office much?' he said suddenly.

'Er, yes,' said Lara, puzzled.

'I presume Alex will want to move down here so she can start work on the houses?'

'Yes, that's right.'

'Do you think she'd be interested in renting that room? I know it's small, and it would take some clearing out, but if you were willing to help . . . '

Lara couldn't believe her ears. She gave him a huge grin as she drew up in the school car park. 'Are you serious?'

'Yes, of course. But if you don't think it would work . . . '

'I think it would be brilliant! I wanted to ask you myself but I didn't want to impose on you. Are you sure you don't mind? That would make two of us staying in your house.'

'It's not going to be forever, is it? And Alex doesn't strike me as the sort of person to go changing my décor without even asking.'

Lara blushed. 'I'm really sorry about that . . . '

'I'm just joking. So, do you want to suggest it to her and see what she says?'

'She'll be delighted,' said Lara firmly. 'I can't thank you enough.' And she leant over and kissed him. She didn't know what made her do it. It wasn't like her at all. It was only on the cheek, and she jumped back immediately and climbed out of the car, but the feel of his warm skin stayed with her.

If that wasn't bad enough, one of the passing fifth years let out a wolf whistle.

Lara could feel herself turning bright red.

'Ignore them,' said Mick with a wink.

It was easy for him to say. She wished she had his self-assurance. Or that she could put him out of her mind as easily as he seemed to put her from his.

It was only that evening Lara remembered the solicitor's words. Despite all the fuss, Ed McAnulty hadn't even put in a bid. Perhaps she should be worrying about Ed rather than Mick. What, indeed, was he playing at?

Two Unexpected Invitations

Mick had two weighty problems on his mind. The more pressing one was whether to tell Lara — and Steve — he had agreed to go out for a pint with Ed on Monday evening. He knew Lara was still suspicious of the man, and he didn't want to upset her. Steve would be absolutely furious, but Mick had decided he couldn't be part of the brothers' feud forever.

His second problem was Lara herself. He had to face up to the fact that he found her very attractive, and yet was making absolutely no progress in getting close to her. If anything, she was more wary of him now than when he had first met her two months ago. She had definitely withdrawn after giving him that kiss on the cheek. He thought over the situation, looking at it from all angles, and the only answer he could come up with was to ask Lara out for a date.

It seemed ridiculous, inviting your own housemate out on a date, but how else was he to get the message through to her that he was interested? Unless he made it blatantly obvious, she would turn the evening into yet another group night out, or pretend she didn't realise it was her company he was after, or cry off due to excess marking. She was far too conscientious a teacher.

For the moment he decided to put both issues from his mind and concentrate on the Friday evening football. It was late April and the lighter nights had caused the number of youths to increase from between twenty and thirty to nearer fifty, and he was struggling to keep them under control. It wasn't that the kids were misbehaving — well, no more than was to be expected — just that there were more of them than he could reasonably keep an eye on.

'This is a nightmare,' he said after

nearly an hour of trying to referee four games simultaneously. He gave two sharp blasts on his whistle and gestured the youths to gather round.

'Right, listen up. I said listen! Ryan, you take this whistle and teams one and two and go to the top field.'

'Er, me?' said Ryan, looking confused. 'Why me?'

'Because I say so. You're the ref and the rest will listen to what you say. Won't they?' Mick narrowed his eyes at the straggling group who looked at each other and shrugged. 'Kyle, you take the ball. OK, off you go. Fifteen minutes each way. And remember, I'm still keeping an eye on you.'

He turned to the remaining youths. On an evening like this Steve could have been really useful, but he was never around when you needed him. Maybe he should see if Ed wanted to rekindle his own interest in football? That was a good reason to have a drink with him.

At that moment a voice from behind

him said, 'Twenty a side, tonight, is it?'
It was Steve.

Mick gave a sigh of relief. 'About time you showed your face. I was relying on you. Don't you know we start at seven? Right, you're reffing this game, take my whistle. Kieran and Liam have already picked sides.'

'I . . . '

'Jamie and Callum, come with me. We'll do a bit of goalie practice. Which I must say is sorely needed.' He dropped his hand on Steve's shoulder and said more quietly, 'You saved my life, mate.' If Steve had been going to protest further, he changed his mind.

Mick led his goalkeeping hopefuls over to a much-vandalised, net-less set of posts. Ryan left his game as they passed him and said, 'Why did you give me the whistle? They never listen to me.'

'Don't you know the rules of the game?'

'Aye, I do so.'

'Well, then. Just sound confident and they'll do what you say.'

* * *

Lara was quietly satisfied with the way things were going. Alex was moving to Loreburn in two weeks' time. The entry date for Ladybank Row was the beginning of May. Her classes were now not only behaving but actually showing signs of having learnt something. And Mick Jensen was keeping his distance, just as she had originally hoped.

So she was unprepared when Mick plumped himself down at the kitchen table late one evening and said, 'Can I ask you something?'

It was the sort of question she hated. If it wasn't important, he would never have started like that. She was immediately on her guard.

'Ye-es?' She fidgeted with her pen. She had been marking Sixth Year Studies essays on global warming. Surprisingly good ones, as it happened.

'You shouldn't be working at this time of night,' he said. 'You work too hard.'

'We had a departmental meeting

earlier. If it's inconvenient for me to use the kitchen table I'm quite happy to work in my room.'

'Of course it's not inconvenient.' He frowned and pushed back the untidy hair.

She waited, giving him the opportunity to ask his question if he wanted to. She hoped he'd hurry up. One more essay and then maybe a hot drink before she went to bed.

Mick adjusted his chair, leant back in it and then leant forwards again. 'It's like this, you see.'

'Mmm?' Lara was starting to feel nervous. Had he changed his mind about Alex having the spare room? Did he want both of them to move out? Maybe things weren't going so well as she had fondly imagined.

'You know the new restaurant that's opened in the Burns' Centre?'

'No.' Lara hadn't been here long enough to be familiar with the eateries of Loreburn.

'Well, it has. And it's supposed to be

good. I thought about trying it.'

'Oh?' Lara wondered why he was telling her this. 'That sounds nice.'

'Does it? So you'll come with me?'

'Well, I . . . ' This was the last thing she had expected. She had been out with Mick and a few others a number of times now, but never just the two of them. 'I don't know.' Keep your distance, keep cool, she chided herself.

Perversely, as her unease grew, Mick seemed to relax. He gave a vague wave of his hand. 'We could go any evening that suits you. Tomorrow? Friday? You decide and I'll fit in.'

Lara tried desperately to think of a good excuse. 'Well, I'm not really sure . . . '

'My treat.' He smiled now, those green eyes warm and encouraging.

Lara didn't smile back. There was no denying it: he was asking her out. Her, on her own. This wasn't a good idea. 'You mean just you and me?'

'Just you and me,' he confirmed, and then a shadow of doubt crossed his tanned face. 'If that's all right?'

'It's very kind of you.' She felt suddenly breathless. She knew she should decline, politely but firmly, yet she was flattered and, yes, tempted, so for a moment she said nothing.

'You don't have to decide now,' he said, and then, 'Well, yes, perhaps you do. Then you won't back out. It's just a meal. Surely we could manage that?'

He was right. It was just a meal. She said slowly, 'It would be nice to go out on Saturday. If you can get a table.'

'I'll phone and find out.'

'OK,' she said weakly. She heard him go straight to the phone. He wasn't going to let this pass. She hadn't considered Mick as someone who made this kind of effort. Maybe she didn't know him as well as she thought? She wasn't sure if this made her more or less uneasy.

* * *

Lara picked up the phone out of habit. She wasn't expecting it to be for her.

Apart from Alex, who would ring?

'Lara, dear, is that you? How lucky to catch you in.'

'Mum?' she said faintly. She wouldn't have called it lucky. Since her trip over to England, when they had failed to meet up, her mother hadn't phoned so often.

'Lara? Is that you? It's a bad line.'

Lara took a deep breath and raised her voice to be heard across the thousands of miles. 'Yes, Mum, it's me. How are you and Dad?'

'We're getting along perfectly well. And how are you?'

'I'm fine too.' Lara was searching her brain for something else to say.

'That's good. How is Alex? Has she moved in with you yet? I have to say, that sounds like an excellent arrangement.'

Lara smiled to herself. Her parents were much happier at the idea of two girls sharing the house with Mick. She didn't tell them that she was rather relieved about the idea herself. If only she hadn't agreed to go out for that meal with him. They chatted about Alex for a while, and about Ladybank Row, which her mother kept referring to as 'all those houses you have taken on' in a worried tone.

Elizabeth's next question came as a shock.

'Lara dear, how would you feel about coming out for your father's retirement party?'

'Me, coming out? To Dubai?' It was a while since Lara had been there. She didn't like the heat or the shiny newness of everything. She knew her parents didn't need her.

'Yes. We're putting on a special party. Your dad has worked for the company for many years. I want it to be a celebration for him. I know he's a little worried about retiring but it can be a positive thing, too, can't it?'

'Er, yes,' said Lara doubtfully. 'So when does he actually retire? I mean, will it be on his birthday?'

'No, not till the end of June. But

we're having the party on the Saturday nearest his birthday.' Her mother gave her the date. 'And you have a long weekend then. I checked on your school website, wasn't that clever of me? I'm getting very good with the Internet. We'll pay your ticket, of course. So do you think you can come?'

Lara shook her head to clear her thoughts. This was more difficult to take in than Mick asking her out for a meal. Her parents rarely invited her to visit. They were, of course, perfectly pleasant if she decided to go (and when had the last time been? Christmas two years ago? Three?) but they never initiated it.

'May's not a good time. All the senior students are doing exams.'

'But surely for a special occasion like this?' Lara remembered now how important social events were for her parents. 'The party will be on the Saturday.'

Lara tried to recall how long the flight was. 'It's a long way to go for such a short time . . . '

'I know, dear. But for this last time? It would mean a lot to us. Of course, after this we'll be moving back to the UK.'

Lara's heart fell. Yes, they were moving back, but not close to her. They had already put in an offer on a bungalow in Devon.

'Please, Lara?'

'I'll think about it. I'll need to look into flights and make sure I can get there and back in the time . . . ' Lara really didn't want to go.

'That would be wonderful, dear. It'll be a very important day for your father, he'll be so pleased if you're there.'

Lara could see that it would be an important day for her father, probably something akin to a knell of doom. She didn't think he'd mind whether she was there or not.

The phone call brought Lara back down to earth, to that cold lonely place that she should have known would always be hers. She couldn't help it.

Even when her mother phoned to invite her to visit she felt rejected. She knew she was rejected. An unwanted only child. They had done their duty by her — just. But she had known for as long as she could remember that she wasn't important. Worse, that she was in the way. She had once overheard her mother telling a friend that Lara's arrival had been a little surprise. Her parents didn't like surprises.

She shrugged angrily. Why go into that now? She had made a life for herself, she didn't need them. Or anyone else, for that matter. Except Alex, who had never let her down, who took her absolutely as she was. She was very lucky to have a friend like that.

Why had she said she would go out with Mick? Her mother's call had come at a good time. She had been thinking, despite everything, of giving Mick a chance. His message of interest had been unmistakable. And she had almost been looking forward to their evening out. Wondering what clothes to wear, which jewellery. All those silly girly things she didn't normally think about.

'Just forget it,' she said aloud to herself. 'There's no point in starting.'

She paced the house, relieved she had it to herself. But how was she to tell Mick she had changed her mind, and get him to agree to it? She was starting to realise behind the laid-back exterior was a kind of dogged determination. It might make it worse, if she withdrew. He'd see her as more of a challenge and push all the harder. Should she just tell him the truth, that she wasn't worth his while? She tried the conversation in her head, but couldn't imagine herself saying the things out loud. Whether he believed her or not, it would be incredibly painful.

The only thing she could think of was to feign illness. She hated to lie, but it was for the best.

Why oh why hadn't she listened to her self-preservation instinct and looked for less troublesome accommodation?

Lara's Project Hits a Snag

Lara eventually decided on a pale lilac dress for Saturday evening, sleeveless and high-necked. She knew it suited her and she liked the fact it wasn't revealing. She chose broad silver hoop earrings to go with it. Gold would have looked warmer, but she was determined to go for the cool look.

She hadn't been able to back out of the arrangement. She was never good at lying, and Mick would have seen through any excuse the minute she made it. And why not have one evening of fun? It wasn't often that a good-looking man invited her out to the newest restaurant in town. And if during the evening he found out for himself that she really wasn't girlfriend material — well, so much the better. Then he wouldn't ask her out again.

Mick had made an effort with his

own appearance. For the first time she could remember he wasn't wearing sports gear or jeans. He had on some pale cream trousers and a soft cotton shirt the colour of moss. You couldn't say he looked exactly smart, when it was slightly creased and the top buttons were undone, but he did look very nice.

Lara smiled a tight little smile. 'Both in our finery.'

He kissed her lightly on the cheek, as though they were meeting for the first time that day and not standing in their own hallway. 'One of us is, at least. You look beautiful.'

Lara shrugged. She never knew how to respond to compliments.

'The taxi should be here any minute.'

'You didn't need to order a taxi. I can drive.'

'So can I.' He grinned, eyes sparkling. 'I mean, I can drive, even though I don't have a car. And I don't see why you should take yours.'

Lara realised, nervously, that this

took away her control over what time they came home. 'It seems a shame to get a taxi for such a short distance.'

'We could walk there, of course.' He looked down at her flimsy shoes. 'Or maybe not. Come on, we're not going to start the evening arguing. Remember, this is my treat. And you know how well-paid teachers are.'

The restaurant was unexpected. A rather narrow room with wide-silled windows set low in the thick walls. The views were across the river to the town centre, which in daylight was hardly picturesque, but in the evening, with the sun dipping low behind the western clouds and the lights beginning to come on, it looked moody and romantic.

The décor was just a little intimidating. The walls were starkly white, the tables bare cubes of dark wood, the glasses and cutlery clearly hand-made.

'It's very, er, impressive,' she said, as the waitress pulled out the heavy chair for her to sit down.

'Not bad, is it?' he agreed. 'Fortunately they do serve beer. What'll you have?'

Lara needed courage and asked for wine. It felt so odd being here like this with Mick, just the two of them.

Mick settled back into his chair, looking as relaxed here as in a crowded pub or on the school playing fields. How she envied him that ease. When their drinks arrived he smiled his intimate smile and said, 'You never did tell me what it was that brought you to Loreburn.'

'I was just looking for a change of scenery.' Lara didn't want to talk about herself.

'Mmm. And why was that?' He took a bite of a freshly baked roll and glanced at her, the question so casual that she might have been tricked into thinking he was hardly listening.

'Nothing in particular.'

'Boyfriend trouble?' said Mick.

'What? No absolutely not.' She took a swallow of wine and said, 'It was my boss that was the final straw, actually.'

'A bad boss can be the pits.'

'She was.' Lara discovered she would rather talk about her awful last job than boyfriends. 'She wasn't very good at her job, and petrified of anyone that might threaten her. I can see that now, but I couldn't at the time. I'd applied for her job, too, and she really resented me. I'm not saying I could have done any better, of course, but . . . '

'Sure you could. You're Miss Totally Wonderful as far as Mr McIntyre is concerned.'

Lara smiled doubtfully. Mick probably meant to be positive, but she felt it put her firmly back in her place — conscientious, hard-working, boring.

'I can certainly see you as a Head of Department. I'm surprised you applied for the job down here. Senior Geography Teacher's not the same, is it? Or are you biding time until a suitable vacancy comes up?'

'No.' Lara took another sip of wine. 'What I realised, watching that awful woman doing the job, was that even if I could do it I didn't want to.'

Mick didn't look convinced. 'You would be really good.'

'But I don't want it, OK?' Lara began to feel the panic she had experienced when Miss Dunlop undermined her so completely. She was grateful when Mick let the subject drop.

'How are you getting on with Mark Frazer?' he asked, referring to the Head of Humanities, as the department of Geography, History and Modern Studies was called at Loreburn High.

'He seems fine, so far.'

'That's good. He's a nice guy.'

She wondered why Mick was smiling at her and then realised it was because she was staring at him. He looked so different in the shirt almost the colour of his eyes. And there was something else. 'You've had your hair cut,' she said.

He grinned, making her heart do an odd little lurch. 'I thought it was time. You must have noticed it was a bit on the long side.'

She gave a half smile, not able to deny this. Whoever had cut the thick blond hair hadn't taken much off. In fact, it was still collar length at the back and not much shorter at the front. It was a lot tidier though.

He gestured to the menu. 'Have you chosen?'

Lara had been so caught up in him, the bright eyes and keen questions, that she hadn't even looked at the sparse and stylish menu. She sighed. This wasn't going at all as she had planned.

'So what do you think of Loreburn so far?' he said, when they had placed their orders. 'Are you enjoying it?'

Lara wondered why the question felt so personal. Other colleagues had asked her that, but from Mick it was different. 'It's a nice town,' she said cautiously. 'And of course, I'm really pleased that we've got Ladybank Row. It's something for Alex and me to get our teeth into.'

'Is it the house or having your friend here that you're so keen on?'

Lara thought carefully. It was a good question. 'Both. They're inter-linked. I love the idea of the houses, and I'm just so relieved that the project is bringing Alex out of herself.'

The food was good and Mick continued to make an effort with the conversation. It was worse than ever, being alone with him like this. The more attractive she realised he was, the more she knew he wasn't for her. On another occasion she might have felt short-changed by the size of the beautifully presented portions, but tonight she had no appetite.

'So do you think you'll be staying in Loreburn long term?'

'Well.' Lara wished he would stop asking her such outright questions. It was difficult to avoid answering without seeming rude. How did she know if she would be staying here long? That had been the intention, but now she thought she would have been safer in Glasgow. There, no-one tried to get too close. 'Maybe.'

She tried to change the subject, to divert him, but he was too quick for her. He wasn't outright nosy, but she found herself giving him some details of her background just to be polite — her parents overseas, the lonely childhood. She kept her answers short, though, and the wry grin that crossed his face at each prim reply did not escape her. See, she wanted to say, I'm very boring, so leave me be.

'Tell me about your family,' she asked eventually. Normally she avoided personal questions, but she had to get him on to another topic. And he was happy enough to talk. He clearly got along well with his parents and two sisters, for all that he mocked them gently as he talked. It might even be that he missed his parents since they moved to Ayr, where his oldest sister was now settled with her husband and two children.

Lara made all the right noises as she listened, not giving any sign of the slow sinking of her heart. She wanted to find something to dislike about Mick Jensen, instead she just realised how different they were.

'I suppose it sounds pretty dull,' he said cheerfully. 'Brought up in Loreburn. Family little more than an hour's drive away even now. I haven't done all that fascinating travel-the-world-stuff that you have done.'

'There are worse places than Loreburn to spend your life.' She meant this as a comfort, a compliment even, but he grinned as though she had been sarcastic.

After that, she kept her contributions to the conversation even more monosyllabic. He was making her nervous. She didn't understand him and he didn't understand her. That was all there was to it. Perhaps the evening on their own was a good thing, if only to make this clear to him.

'When do you think you'll be able to move into Ladybank Row?' asked Mick as they ordered coffee. She wondered if there was a note of tension creeping into his voice.

'As soon as we can. I mean, it's very nice at your place, but we don't want to presume . . . '

'As I said before, it's no bother. I wasn't asking because I wanted you to move out.'

'I'm sure we're in your way though, especially as there will be two of us soon. It can't be like it was when you shared with Steve.'

'Believe me, it's nothing like it was when I shared with Steve.'

'That's what I mean. I know I said I'd only stay for a month or so and it's already nearly three . . . '

'Lara, if I wanted you to move out, I'd say so, OK? I was just asking about Ladybank Row out of interest. Stop apologising, OK?'

Lara was glad when the waitress brought their bill and it was time to go home. She had known coming out for this meal would be a mistake. It was one she would make sure she didn't repeat.

The evening hadn't ended the way Mick had hoped, although he wasn't quite sure why that was.

He had tried and tried to get Lara to talk to him, and sometimes he thought he was succeeding. Then she would back off again, withdraw with that cool politeness of hers, until he wanted to scream with frustration. Perhaps the meal hadn't been such a good idea. It seemed to have put her on edge.

Mick decided to forget Lara and go for a run. He might even pop in and see Steve. A bit of uncomplicated male company would make a nice change.

As he jogged along the road near Steve's new place he was surprised to see Ryan O'Donnell coming out of one of the terraced houses. He hadn't thought of this as Ryan's part of town.

'Hiya, how you doing?' The boy jumped guiltily at the sound of his voice, not a good sign. 'You did well at football Friday night.'

'Oh, hmm, hi.'

Mick examined him, wishing he had

time to take more interest. Ryan had grown in the last few months, he was gangly and far too pale, with more spots than ever.

'Have you found a job yet?'

'You sound like a social worker. Not likely, is it?' The boy sniffed and made to move off.

'You could always consider going to the Tech, like we discussed. They do really good PE and leisure activity courses. There're lots of opportunities for work there . . .'

'Aye, right. I can just see me working at one of those posh gyms.'

'Just a thought, Ryan.'

'Look, got to go, OK?' The boy sloped off, shivering in his too-thin jacket.

Mick watched him for a moment. These kids really needed someone to make an effort for them. Why was he doing this football training if he couldn't give them a hundred and ten percent? Ryan had a point, perhaps he was as bad as the social workers.

Playing at helping but never carrying anything through. What these kids needed was a goal. If he couldn't find them jobs, at least he could give them something to focus on, like a football tournament. Now, that was an idea.

⋆　⋆　⋆

Lara was happy. She was happy. She had a job that was mostly satisfying, with a good bunch of kids and a fairly motivated staff. She had the Ladybank Row project that was so big it frightened her, but at least it guaranteed she wouldn't be bored for months, if not years, to come. And her good friend had arrived and they were taking the first steps on the houses.

So she wouldn't think about the other things: her mother's invitation to Dubai, Alex's eating too much, or Mick. If she didn't think about any of those things she would be fine.

They would need to get workmen in to do the major jobs at Ladybank Row, but in the meantime Lara and Alex decided to get on with a bit of clearing out themselves. The first weekend after Alex's arrival they got really stuck in.

Alex, who much preferred being outside, set to clearing the rampant undergrowth in the gardens. Lara decided to make a start on the bedroom in Number One.

She found that demolition work could actually be quite good fun. She put all her weight down on the end of the crowbar and watched with satisfaction as the side wall of the flimsy built-in cupboard came away. 'We're building something here,' she said to herself, and smiled at her own joke.

They had decided to concentrate on one of the four houses to begin with. She was stripping all the rooms of the end terrace, now known as Number One. During the week, Alex had started to rip up the downstairs carpets and attack the shabby kitchen cupboards.

A persistent drizzle drove Alex back inside, which pleased Lara. She didn't think working on the gardens was really a priority at the moment.

'Can you help me carry all this stuff downstairs?' she said, indicating the pile of boards that had once been a wardrobe.

'We need to get a skip,' said Alex.

'You're right.' Lara should have thought of that. 'I'll order one on Monday.'

'You'll be working. I'll order one,' said Alex. Lara stared at her. Alex didn't usually take the initiative. Now she carried on stolidly clearing away the debris, as though what she had said was nothing out of the ordinary.

Then Alex said something that surprised her even more.

'How are things going with you and your Mick?' she asked, making Lara jump. It was two weeks since the meal and she definitely didn't want to think about it.

'He's not 'my Mick', don't be ridiculous.'

'He's really nice, Lara.' Alex glanced

up once, then pushed her long plait back over her shoulder and continued with her work.

'Of course he's nice. He's letting us both stay in his house. But that's all it is.'

'I think he likes you,' said Alex. Fortunately she didn't push the point and Lara was happy to leave it there.

The problem was, it made her think about Mick even more than she had been doing already. She had learnt something about this man she would never have suspected when she first met him. She already knew the scruffy clothes and casual manner were a front for a conscientious teacher. But even more impressive was the football coaching that he did voluntarily and unpaid, every Friday evening.

Mick hadn't told her about that, of course, but Sandy Woods had mentioned it in passing. Everything Lara learnt about Mick made her respect him a little more. It was a shame she really wasn't the right sort of person to go out with him.

★ ★ ★

The following day a roofer came round to Ladybank Row to give them a quote for the work that needed doing. His visit made Lara forget all about Mick: it gave her something much more worrying to think about. They discovered the reason Ed McAnulty hadn't put in a bid on the houses.

Lara knew the roof at Ladybank Row was one of the first things that would need attention, and she had been pleased to find a roofer willing to come around and give her a quote on a Sunday. She hoped it wasn't going to be too expensive. She and Alex waited nervously as Gary Glover crawled slowly through the attic spaces, pried up ridge tiles, explored the venting, and then came down to give his report.

'Did you have a survey done on this place?'

Lara could tell that what he had to say wasn't good news.

'Yes,' she said. 'Not a full structural

report, just the valuation type.'

'Aye, thought as much.'

'Is there a problem?' said Lara. 'Is the roof not sound?'

Mr Glover was a small sandy-haired man of indeterminate age. His responses were as slow as his methodical examination of the properties. 'Some of the sarking needs replacing, but that's not a big job. And a few of the slates are blown, but again it won't be a great load of work to sort that.'

'So what's the problem?' asked Alex anxiously.

'You see the wee corrugated iron roofs, on the lean-to?'

'Yes. We know we've got to do something about those. The iron is rusted, it'll have to go.'

'It's no just the iron that'll have to go. It's the asbestos underneath you need to worry about. Nasty stuff, asbestos.'

'Asbestos?' said Lara, horrified. 'But why wasn't this picked up on the survey?'

'It would have been,' said the man

laconically. 'If you'd had a full survey.'

Lara's thoughts were in turmoil. Asbestos was poisonous, wasn't it? It was dangerous — and expensive to get rid of. Why hadn't anyone noticed it until now?

'Can see why they put it there, like,' said the man. 'Good insulation and in those days they wouldn't worry about all this Health and Safety. You can't have it now, though. It'll have to go.'

'Is it white asbestos or blue?' said Alex. Her health studies had obviously come in useful here. 'It looks like white to me.'

'White, of course, which is not so bad. Still, it'll have to be done right. I can give you a quote to remove it myself, but it won't be cheap.'

'We'd be grateful if you would,' said Lara, trying not to sound as worried as she felt. 'You've got our address, haven't you? Can you send it there? We'll let you know what we decide to do.'

She should have known something

like this was going to happen. They hadn't even started the building work before they hit this first snag. What else was going to go wrong? Lara felt tense and nervous as she hadn't done in months. This was going to delay them and could seriously eat into their profits. It was all her fault, for having involved Alex in her crazy plans. She was sure Ed McAnulty would have known about the asbestos, and would be expecting them to trip up at the first hurdle.

Lara Confronts Her Parents

Lara had decided. She didn't want to go to Dubai so she wouldn't. She dialled the number and waited for the slow connection to be made. Glancing out through the window beside the front door she saw the little willow tree tossing its soft green leaves in the summer breeze. She liked these early summer evenings. She was very glad she was here and not in the searing heat of the desert.

'It's Lara,' she said when her mother answered.

'Lara?' Her mother sounded sleepy and Lara remembered belatedly that Dubai was a few hours ahead of Scotland. It would be late evening there. 'I hope I didn't wake you,' she said. 'I'll be quick. I just wanted to say I really don't think it'll be possible for me to come out for the retirement party.'

'Oh Lara, that's such a shame.' Lara was used to that tone from her mother. One of disappointment. She nearly offered to go out some other time, to try and make it up to them, but held her tongue. She was sure her mother didn't really want to see her. She just needed her presence, for the sake of form. It was time Lara stopped wishing otherwise.

Then her mother said, 'Please, Lara.' And she sounded so desperate that before she knew it Lara was softening.

'I didn't want you to waste your money for such a short visit but if you really want . . . '

'Oh Lara, do come. We really want you. Don't we, Derek?'

Lara heard a mutter in the background that sounded like agreement.

'If you're sure . . . '

'Absolutely. Darling, this is wonderful.' Her mother sounded wide awake now. 'I'll get on to the travel agent first thing tomorrow.'

Lara shook her head as she replaced

the telephone receiver. She couldn't believe she had just agreed to do the very thing she had decided against.

★　★　★

Mick had felt Lara was relaxing with him over the last week or so. Did that mean she did enjoy his company? But if so, why did she find it so difficult to show it? He had pondered this problem during Sunday morning, but hadn't come to any conclusion.

So now he had decided to beard her in what he saw as her own territory, and headed over to Ladybank Row. He collected his friend, Steve, on the way, for moral support.

'See if you can get Alex out of the way and give me some time on my own with Lara,' he said.

'Like that, is it?'

Mick eyed his friend, wondering if he would regret opening his heart to him. He decided he would. In any case, there wasn't time. They passed the station, the waste ground, the garage and warehouse, and rounded the corner into Ladybank Row. It was strange he had never noticed before what a quiet little place this was, right in the centre of town.

Unfortunately things didn't work out as he had hoped. Steve and he were immediately roped into carrying the piles of carpets and other rubbish into the garden in preparation for a bonfire. He was alone with one or other of the girls for a minute now and then, it was never long enough to start a conversation. Lara and Alex were both grubby and pink-faced from their exertions, but he was impressed at how much they had done.

'You're going to have two problems with this fire,' said Steve, as they dragged the last bit of plyboard on to the pile. 'Firstly, no matches to light it with. Secondly, no fire lighters to make sure the blaze takes.'

He had his hands thrust into the pockets of his jeans and was watching the girls with amusement. He was more like his brother than he would have cared to admit, in his attitude to women and building work.

Lara checked her watch. It was already after five. 'I should have thought of that. Will there be a shop open at this time on a Saturday?'

'Of course there will,' said Steve. 'I'll go if you want.' Mick smiled gratefully, especially when his friend added to Alex, 'Why don't you come too? You can help me carry back some bottles of water, I think we all deserve a drink.'

Alex looked surprised, but to Mick's delight she agreed.

That just left him and Lara. Mick perched himself on a broken down garden bench. 'Come on, take a break. Looks like you've been hard at it all day.' He smiled encouragingly and gestured to the other end of the bench. Lara chose to sit on an up-ended petrol can instead.

She took a deep breath and looked around. 'It looks like it, er, might rain, later.' Despite sharing a house, it was the first time the two of them had been alone for a while, and she looked uneasy.

'Might, might not. The forecast was mixed. It's going to be worse tomorrow, which is a shame. I've got the youth football practice in the evening.'

'Oh, football.' She turned, her attention caught. 'I thought you did that on a Friday?'

'Aye, most of the time. But I'm thinking of entering a couple of teams in a competition, and they need some extra practice.' And some extra discipline, he thought.

'That'd be great. Great for them, I mean. I hear they're . . . not the easiest group of kids.'

'No.' Mick grinned briefly. 'Not exactly kids, either, but still at the stage where they need something to occupy them, to keep them out of mischief.'

'The Council should fund projects like yours.'

'They run other schemes. Boys like

these wouldn't go if it was official. And especially not if they had to pay.'

'So you do it in your own time, for nothing.'

Mick shrugged. It was no big deal as far as he was concerned, although anything that made Lara look at him with approval in his dark eyes had to be positive. Now the mood had been set, he didn't have time to waste or Steve and Alex would be back and he'd be no further forward.

'You know that meal out we had,' he said.

'Ye-es.'

'Would you like to do that again some time?'

She blushed, just a faint darkening of her creamy skin, but noticeable all the same. 'I don't think we should. It was lovely, of course, but so expensive, I wouldn't want to waste your money.'

'You could invite me out, if you wanted.'

'Oh.' The blush deepened. It was fascinating to know that you could break through that reserve and he pressed his advantage.

'But only if you wanted to, of course. Would you want to?'

She looked down, ostensibly examining a broken nail. 'I could cook you a meal at the house.'

'But it's not the same, is it? There's always someone else around. Like now. The others will be back in a minute. I'm looking to spend some time with you on my own.'

Lara looked at her watch, as though she wished the others were already there. He held his breath and waited. He didn't know how much to say, how much to push. He didn't want to drive her further away, but so far this approach was having better results than the politer one. 'Lara?'

'Ah. Um.'

'We could go out a few times. Give it a try. See if we, er, like each other.'

She shot him a quick look from below dark lashes. 'Do you want to?'

Of course he wanted to! But he also

wanted to know what she wanted. He put out a hand and took one of hers. She wasn't quite far enough away to prevent it. 'I want to. How about you?'

'I don't know,' she said, with a sigh, but she let her hand rest in his, slim and cool.

She laughed breathlessly. 'You don't want to do that. They're filthy.'

'Not nearly as filthy as I would be if I'd been doing what you've been doing all day.'

She smiled at him, and then jumped as the sound of footsteps could be heard, and Steve and Alex appeared around the side of the house.

Lara jumped up. 'Cold drinks, that's a great idea. I'll go and get mugs, shall I?' She hurried away, leaving Mick with no idea if he had made progress or not.

* * *

Lara was still mulling over Mick's words the following day. He had almost convinced her that he was genuine, that he liked her and yet, and yet, she still couldn't make up her mind what to do next.

Then her mother phoned on the Monday morning to confirm her flight details for Dubai and she decided to make no decision until that trip was over. She thought Mick looked rather downhearted when she told him of her plans, but Alex was pleased. She seemed to think it would be good for Lara to spend time with her parents. Just because she had never known her own parents, and had adored her gran, she seemed to think family was important. Lara decided it was easiest not to disagree.

It seemed no time at all before she was on her way to Glasgow airport to catch the flight. Alex was driving her, in Lara's car. Mick had offered to come too but Lara had refused politely. She couldn't see why anyone would want to spend four hours in a car if they didn't have to.

'Will you be all right without me?' Lara asked her friend for the umpteenth time. Alex seemed much brighter these days, but she couldn't help worrying.

'Of course. I'll be working on Ladybank Row. I'll be fine.'

'That's good,' said Lara, although she wasn't quite sure she believed her friend.

'You'll give your parents a chance, won't you?' said Alex suddenly.

'Goodness, what on earth do you mean?'

'This must be important to them. They're so happy you're going,' said Alex.

'Mmm,' said Lara, still not convinced.

She thought about Alex's words during the long hours of the flight. Alex might like to think family was important, but despite their years of friendship she didn't understand Lara's situation. Her parents didn't dote on her as Alex's gran had done on her granddaughter. And yet, and yet — they were paying her air fare, weren't they? They did seem to want to see her this time. She sighed, feeling this was a conundrum she would never solve.

★ ★ ★

As the chauffeur turned the large car into their compound, Elizabeth gave a smile of relief. The party had gone well. Derek had been praised and rewarded just as he should have been. And, best of all, Lara had been there to enjoy it with them.

As they climbed the broad marble steps to the house she touched her daughter's arm. 'I'm so glad you came.'

'It's been very nice,' said her daughter, cautious as always. She looked so beautiful. Her short dark hair was lustrous. She was wearing the silk dress of midnight blue Elizabeth had had such fun choosing for her, and looked as smart now as she had done at the beginning of the evening.

'Time for a nightcap?' suggested Derek.

Elizabeth saw her daughter hesitate and held her breath. Lara was leaving first thing in the morning, so this was the last chance for the three of them to be together.

'I wouldn't mind a cup of tea,' said Lara at length.

'I'll put the kettle on,' said Elizabeth quickly. The maid would long since have retired to her room. 'You two make yourselves comfortable in the lounge.'

'We'll sit on the patio,' said Derek. 'It's cool enough at this time of night.'

Elizabeth hurried to lay a tray of tea things for herself and her daughter. She knew she should be glad Lara and her father had the chance to talk together, but it made her nervous. Derek had never been good at communicating with young people, and after the emotion of the evening he would probably be feeling tense.

When she joined them on the dimly

lit patio neither was speaking.

'It was a lovely party, wasn't it?' she said brightly.

It was Lara who answered. 'They did you proud, Dad. They're obviously going to miss you.'

'Hmm,' said Derek. He was never good at accepting compliments, but Lara wasn't to know that. She would think he was merely impatient. 'If they think I've so much to offer, it would be nice if they gave me another year's contract.'

Elizabeth's heart fell. 'But Derek, we've agreed we're leaving. We've bought the house in Devon . . . '

'We could rent it out, no problem.'

'Mum has been looking forward to moving there,' said Lara, taking her mother by surprise with her vehement tone. 'She wants the fun of doing up her own place. I can understand that, now I've got Ladybank Row.'

Derek grunted. His thick hair, once as dark as Lara's, was now completely white. In the soft light it was hard to see the expression on his face. 'I've said it before and I'll say it again, I don't know why you put all your money into a place like that. Sounds like the buildings are derelict. What do a couple of girls know about doing up derelict buildings?'

'They're not derelict,' said Lara. 'Perhaps if you came over to see for yourself you would know that.'

'I've been busy. And I've heard enough from your mother to form my judgment.'

'Mum hasn't seen them either.' Lara put her cup down on the saucer with a clatter. She sounded angry. 'When was the last time either of you visited me? But you still think you can offer comment on the way I do things. I don't know why. What is it to you if I have taken on too much? I won't come rushing to you for help. Because I'll know you're too busy.'

'Lara!' protested Elizabeth. This was awful. Derek disliked arguments and would particularly hate to hear such words from his daughter.

'I don't know what you're talking about, young lady,' said Derek, his voice edgy.

Suddenly there seemed to be no stopping Lara. 'It's not just me,' she said. 'What about Mum? You didn't even bother to go over to Devon with her to help her choose the house. Now you'll probably say she made the wrong decision, but it isn't her fault, is it? You're always criticising her. But if you don't make the effort to involve yourself then what can you expect?'

'Lara,' said Elizabeth again. Part of her was touched by her daughter's concern, but mostly she was just horrified at the angry words being exchanged.

'I've said enough, I know.' Lara rose to her feet. 'Don't worry, I'll be gone tomorrow and you probably won't see me again for years.'

She swept through the open patio doors and disappeared.

Elizabeth put her hand out tentatively to her husband. 'It's probably just all the excitement, she doesn't mean . . .'

Derek twitched his arm away. She could tell he was upset. He finished his nightcap in silence and they too retired to bed.

Mick Tries to Win Over Lara

'Something's not right,' said Lara. It was the Saturday following her trip to Dubai. She was keen to busy herself with practicalities and had headed immediately over to Ladybank Row. One of the first things they had done when they took possession of the houses was to put proper locks on the doors but this time it opened without needing a key. 'It's not been locked properly.'

'Maybe I forgot,' said Alex doubtfully, but Lara continued to look about suspiciously. It didn't feel right. She sniffed the air, as though that could tell her something, but all she could smell was the familiar scent of damp and plaster.

'Gary Glover's people were the last ones here,' said Alex. 'I told them to lock up when they left.' Still Lara said nothing. 'It's good to have the work on those roofs started, isn't it?'

'Yes,' said Lara, wondering why she still fell ill at ease. Alex was right, it was a massive relief to know the asbestos was being removed. Gary Glover had come in with a very reasonable quote and they had given the contract to him. He and his men had started the previous week, carefully kitted out in face masks and white overalls, as though involved in some surgical operation.

Maybe they were the ones who hadn't locked up correctly, but she still felt concerned. Or perhaps she just wanted something else to worry about, instead of her parents. Or Mick.

She had managed to avoid Mick since her return. She knew it was pathetic, but if she didn't see him she could pretend their friendship was just that, an easy friendship. Maybe soon he would realise it was best if it remained that way. Lara's visit to her parents had reminded her that happy families weren't for her.

The girls continued the work Alex had been doing all week, stripping back the house to its bare bones. Once Lara got involved in the job she forgot about the unlocked door. She even forgot about Mick, most of the time, until he phoned on her mobile, which was most unusual.

'Are you at Ladybank?' he said in his easy way. 'I thought you might be. OK if I bring someone round to see you?'

'I suppose so,' said Lara, mystified. It was far more typical of Mick to just turn up. 'Who is it?'

'Wait and see. We'll be there in fifteen minutes.'

Lara frowned. She presumed it wasn't Steve, or he wouldn't have phoned to warn her. What if it was Ed? The thought of Ed's glowering presence filled her with dread. These were her houses. Well, hers and Alex's. She didn't want him anywhere near.

It was a relief, therefore, when Mick arrived with a slim youth in tow. He looked sixteen or seventeen but Lara didn't recognise him from school. She would have remembered those eyebrow piercings.

'Hi there,' she said when Mick brought the boy through to the kitchen where Lara was working.

'This is Ryan,' said Mick, slapping the boy on the shoulder. 'One of my more promising footballers. Used to be at the High, but that was before your time.'

'Nice to meet you,' said Lara.

'Umm,' said the youth.

'Ryan mentioned last time I saw him that he wasn't working at the moment and I remembered you said you could do with an extra pair of hands here. So I asked him if he'd like to help you out and here we are.'

Ryan was looking uncomfortable. Lara guessed he hadn't volunteered to 'help her out'. But if Mick had made the effort to bring the boy here he must be keen to get him involved.

'It wouldn't be anything permanent,' she said cautiously.

'He's just looking for some casual work. He's stronger than he looks and he'll do what he's told. Well, most of the time.'

Lara considered the youth. She knew all too many boys like Ryan. Very few of those from difficult backgrounds continued at school past sixteen, whether they were capable or not. It was such a shame.

'We could give it a try, see how it goes,' she said. If Mick had made this much effort they had to give the boy a chance. 'I'll have to see what Alex thinks, but I'm sure she'd appreciate a hand during the week when I'm not around. Why don't you come by at nine tomorrow and we can see?'

'That's brilliant,' said Mick, beaming. 'How about it, then, Ryan? That OK with you?'

'Aye, I suppose.' The boy looked at Lara, but didn't meet her eyes. 'I'll see you tomorrow, then.'

'Nine o'clock remember,' said Lara. 'Don't be late.'

The boy trudged out and the house was silent for a moment. Lara felt she'd made a momentous decision rather too quickly.

'I'm really grateful,' said Mick. 'I hope you don't think I've imposed on you? He's not a bad lad and he's just . . . going nowhere at the moment. I've been at my wits end wondering what to do with him and when I thought of this it seemed ideal.'

Lara was impressed by the interest he took in these kids. But she felt she had to be cautious. 'We'll see how he turns out,' she said. 'It's up to him now.'

'I know. But I still can't thank you enough. And since I'm here, how about putting me to some use?'

'If you're sure . . . ? There's a wheelbarrow out there, you could start by giving Alex a hand in the garden. I'll make some tea.'

The warm feeling stayed with Lara for the rest of the afternoon. Mick was a genuinely nice man. He made an effort for these kids. He had said he

liked her and wanted to go out with her
— why not give him a chance?

Later, when they had once again lit a
bonfire and were watching the sparks
race up into the darkening sky she
went, of her own accord, to stand
beside him. Alex was on the opposite
side of the flames. Lara took a deep
breath and said quickly, 'I'm free on
Tuesday night. I wondered if I could
invite you out for a drink?'

He froze, saying nothing, and she
wanted to turn and run. She actually
made a small movement away from
him, trying desperately to think of some
way of retracting her words.

'That sounds like a great idea to me.'

'Oh, er, good.' She felt breathless.

'It's a date then,' he said and squeezed
her hand. He seemed really pleased.
Maybe this wasn't a mistake.

* * *

Ironically, Lara didn't see Mick at all
on the Sunday as she was busy with

Ryan at Ladybank Row and he was at a football tournament. On Monday their times in the staff room didn't seem to coincide. She didn't think he was trying to avoid her. By the time she came home Mick had gone out, presumably to do more football coaching.

Lara wasn't sorry to retire to bed before he returned. She really didn't know how to act towards him. They had held hands for a few minutes, that was all. She was behaving more like seventeen than twenty-seven.

Tuesday was much the same, although Mick did manage to say when passing her on one of the long school corridors, 'Still OK for tonight?' which made her want to sink into the ground in case one of the students overheard. She managed to nod stiffly and move on. Even that brief exchange caused giggles and nudges amongst the teenage girls behind her. She wondered why she had ever wanted to teach.

She stayed a little late at school once again, to make sure everything was ready for the next morning, and it was nearly six by the time she got home. She had thought everything through. What she would wear, where they would go, how she would behave.

When she walked in the door Mick shot out of the sitting room with his mobile in one hand. 'Thank goodness. I was just about to call you.'

'Yes?'

He looked harassed, very unusual for Mick, his face tense and pinched. 'I'm sorry, but I'm going to have to call off tonight.'

'Oh. Well, that's OK.' She felt her stomach plummet. This was one scenario she had not foreseen.

He took her arm and shook it lightly. 'Temporarily, that's all. I've got to go over to Ayr.'

'Ayr?' said Lara, feeling stupid. She had been so keyed up for the evening she was finding it hard to take this in. Why would he go to Ayr?

'My father's not well. He's been taken in to hospital. It's a suspected heart attack. They say he's out of danger but I need to go.'

'Yes, of course. Goodness. I hope he's OK.'

'He'll probably be fine. My sister phoned about ten minutes ago.' His mobile rang and he answered it instantly. 'Yes? Steve, hi. I can? Great, I'll be right over.' He gave Lara a quick smile. 'I'm borrowing Steve's car. I'm sorry about this.'

'That's OK,' said Lara, remembering to breathe and feeling better for it. 'It's perfectly understandable. I'm just sorry this has happened.'

'So am I.'

They looked at each other in silence for a moment, then Mick's mobile gave that beep that indicates a text message coming in. 'That's my sister giving the ward number. I really must go.'

'Yes.' Lara realised she was still standing in the doorway and moved aside to let him pass.

* * *

Ryan was proving to be surprisingly useful. He wasn't sociable and didn't seem to have much initiative, but he did turn up on time and do more or less what he was asked. His accent was so broad that even Alex, who had been brought up in the area, had difficulty understanding him, but as he spoke little that wasn't much of a problem. The extra pair of hands meant that the stripping out of the houses was continuing apace. After only three days of his input they needed a second skip, which Lara felt was definite progress.

It was good to have something positive to hold on to, because she had heard nothing from Mick since his hasty departure on Tuesday. She knew his father was no worse, because Mr McIntyre mentioned it in passing, so surely Mick could have made the effort to get in touch? It just proved what she had known all along, that he wasn't the reliable kind.

When her phone rang at break on Thursday she thought it was Mick calling at last. Instead, she found herself speaking to young Ryan.

'There's a man here from the Council. He's asking for you.' He sounded upset.

Lara frowned, still trying to take in the fact it wasn't Mick. 'What does he want?'

'I don't know. You've to come round now.'

'I can't, I'm teaching,' said Lara. What on earth was going on? 'Where's Alex? Can't she speak to him?'

'She's not here. Look, you've to come, right? It's not me he wants.' And with that he finished the call.

Lara tried to think what classes she had next and realised, to her relief, that she actually had a free period straight after break. If she was quick she could get to Ladybank Row and back before she needed to teach again. She grabbed her bag and car keys and went to tell Mark Frazer where she was going.

As she parked the car Lara told herself to calm down. It would be something and nothing. A boy like Ryan had no doubt been in trouble with officials more than once. He would panic when approached by a man in a suit. She'd sort this out and be back at school in two minutes.

She straightened her skirt and took a deep breath as she went to greet the stranger who had appeared around the side of Number One.

She proffered her hand. 'I'm Lara Mason. I believe you were looking for me?'

'If you're the owner of this place then yes, I am.' He was a severe-looking man in his mid-fifties with receding grey hair and a grey suit. Nothing about him was welcoming. He introduced himself in a clipped accent. It turned out he wasn't from the Council but from SEPA, the Scottish Environmental Protection Agency. He produced an intimidating little photocard to prove it.

'How can I help you?' said Lara, mystified.

'I'm here to serve an infringement

notice on you. In connection with the asbestos that has been removed from the property.' He flipped open a file and consulted his notes. 'There has been a contravention of the Landfill Scotland Regulations 2003. This is a very serious matter.'

'What regulations? We've arranged to have asbestos removed. We knew that having it in a house didn't comply with current building regulations, or whatever, and . . . '

'Building regulations are of no concern to me. It is waste disposal that comes within my remit. I wonder if you are aware, young lady, that you can be reported to the procurator fiscal for not disposing of such products appropriately?'

'But,' said Lara, her heart sinking. The man was so intimidating, so sure he was right. 'I think there must have been a misunderstanding. We've employed a contractor to remove the asbestos. I know he had all the correct certificates, I saw them myself.' She racked her brains, trying to think how this could have happened. It hadn't even occurred to her to ask to see the certificates but Gary Glover had insisted on showing them.

'Not according to the evidence,' said the man coldly. 'How do you explain a significant amount of white asbestos fly-tipped into the Kinner Water above Dunmuir? A quiet enough little place but luckily someone spotted it. The water course has already been seriously polluted. There are livestock in the adjacent fields. What on earth were you thinking of?'

'But,' said Lara again. 'But this can't be right. It can't be us.'

'I'm afraid it is. I've just taken a sample from one of the roofs and it matches our find exactly. I'm putting a prohibition notice on any further work on these properties until we find out exactly what has been going on. I suppose we should be thankful it wasn't blue asbestos. You do know that asbestos is classified as potentially dangerous to human life? Now, I'll need the name of this contractor of yours, and your personal details, and . . . '

Lara felt ill with the shock. She managed to provide the information requested and waited for the man to leave. Then she went in search of Ryan, to see if he could shed any light on what was going on, but he was nowhere to be found. When she thought to check the time she realised with horror she had already missed most of the lesson before lunch. She hurried to her car, but there was really no point in dashing back now. The damage would be done. Mr McIntyre would not be impressed.

She gave a shuddering sigh as she sank into the driver's seat. She needed to catch her breath and sort out her scattered thoughts. This was a nightmare. How could they have been served a contravention notice? She, Lara, who was always so particular to stick to the rules? Things like this didn't happen to her.

She would have to find Alex and see what she thought of the disaster.

Somehow they would have to sort this mess out. But for a moment she needed to be on her own, to fight back the tears of anger at the news and the way the man had broken it to her. Where did this leave their plans for Ladybank Row now?

★ ★ ★

Mick was in a quandary. His father was on the mend, thank goodness, but it had been touch and go for a while. Mick felt some pressure to stay on in Ayr. The old man appreciated having family around, as did his mother and sister. He liked being with them, but it wasn't a good time to be away from home. Mid week, mid term, was busy enough and now he was stuck fifty miles away.

He thought about Lara more than once but there was nothing he could do now about their cancelled date. She would understand.

So he was more than a little surprised

when he saw her across the staff room on the Friday morning, his first day back, and she swung around and left the room before he could get to her. Gosh, what had he done now? He tried to find her at lunchtime but she seemed to have disappeared.

He went to the school office to check Lara's timetable and found she was free the next to last period. Mick was supposed to be taking a group of fourth years for rugby, but they could wait a few minutes for once.

He settled himself in the corner of the staff room where Lara usually sat, flicking through the fixtures schedule for the next few weeks, but mostly keeping his eye on the door. A couple of members of staff asked about his dad but he took care not to get into long conversations. It would be just his luck that Lara would vanish if he didn't catch her as soon as she appeared. He was just starting to think she wasn't coming, it was so long since the bell had rung, when the door was pushed open and there she was.

Her arms were so full of exercise books she was almost at the table before she noticed Mick.

'Hi there,' he said.

'Oh. Hi.' She looked around for somewhere else to sit. Even after almost a day's teaching, with her arms full of books, she looked neat and tidy, the dark hair in place, the pale blue summer dress spotless. His heart gave a little kick at how beautiful she was.

He stood up hastily and took the books from her. 'You shouldn't carry so much around, I've never known anyone to do as much marking as you do.'

'We're doing weather at the moment,' she said vaguely. 'Lots of diagrams and things, you know.' The second bell went, meaning that the next lesson had begun. 'Shouldn't you be teaching now?'

'Yes.' Now, how had she known that? He felt more hopeful, taking it as a sign of her interest in him. 'But I wanted a word with you.'

'Ah.' She looked down and then collected herself and said, 'Sorry, I should have asked. How's your father doing?'

'He's much better, thank goodness. That's what I wanted to talk to you about. I'm staying here this evening and I wondered whether we could resurrect our . . . date?'

She was still looking down. 'I don't know. We've got a bit of a problem at Ladybank Row and I need to talk to Alex.' From what he could see of her face her expression was fixed. 'Haven't you got football training?'

'Steve's doing it. I arranged that because I didn't know if I'd be back from Ayr.'

'I'm glad your dad's getting better,' she said again, her tone still stilted.

'Lara, what's wrong?'

'Nothing.'

'Look, I really need to go. The kids'll be out on the field already. Can we discuss it tonight?'

When she didn't answer he put out a hand and raised her chin so she had to meet his eyes. He knew a couple of people were staring, but it couldn't be helped. 'Please?'

'Why didn't you phone?' she said, the words seeming to come out of their own accord. 'Sorry, forget it, stupid of me.'

'Phone?' It hadn't occurred to him to phone during the long, anxious days. 'I never thought,' he said. Had she expected him to? No wonder she was upset with him. 'I'm sorry.'

She gazed at him for a few moments, her dark eyes still cautious. He wanted to take her in his arms but he couldn't do that here. There would be enough staff room gossip as it was.

'I'm really sorry,' he said again.

'It's fine, no problem,' she said.

She seemed to have relaxed ever so slightly, but he didn't have time to pursue this now. He had just seen Mr McIntyre go past the windows in the direction of the playing fields. Wouldn't you just know it?

'I've got basketball training till five

and then I'm free. We could go out for a drink, surely? Wait for me at the house. Please?'

'OK,' she said, with a faint sigh.

As he jogged outside he couldn't help grinning. If she minded his not phoning that much it must mean something, mustn't it?

But You're Not My Boyfriend

Lara stood before the long mirror in her bedroom, trying to decide what to wear. It was difficult as she didn't know where they were going, or even what kind of impression she was trying to make. And also, despite how momentous this date had previously seemed, it now occupied only half her thoughts. She was waiting for Alex to come home, so they could discuss the prohibition notice that had put paid to any progress at Ladybank Row, and why on earth Gary Glover had turned out to be so unreliable.

She had just decided on black linen trousers and a silky green top when Alex arrived. Lara wondered where she had been, she no longer had the excuse of the Ladybank Row to hide herself away in. Lara supposed they could continue work on the gardens, but Alex didn't seem inclined to do so.

'I'm up here,' she called from the top of the stairs. 'Come and talk to me.' She shouldn't really be going out with Mick. It was ridiculous, when she had so much to discuss with her friend.

'I tried to phone the solicitor but I couldn't get an answer,' said Alex, looking guilty.

'That's OK, I spoke to him myself,' said Lara. She hoped this difficulty wasn't going to push Alex back into her lethargy. 'I told him we haven't done anything wrong, but he says we need to be able to prove it.'

'How do we do that, if Gary Glover was taking our asbestos and dumping it illegally? Aren't we somehow responsible?' Alex chewed her lip, looking more worried than ever.

Lara had been thinking much the same. She had looked at the sort of fines they might be liable for, and they were massive. With a cashflow that was already under strain, this was something they could really do without. She also hated the stigma of having broken the law. And goodness knew how much more delay to their timetable.

'We did see his certificates,' said Lara. 'But they obviously didn't mean anything.'

'His men seemed very professional,' said Alex. 'They were really careful.'

'We're going to find Mr Glover first thing tomorrow morning,' said Lara. 'I don't know why he won't return our calls.' The very fact that he didn't made her all the more worried.

'I'll leave you now,' said Alex, looking pleased to be able to slip away. 'I can see you're going out, I don't want to hold you up.'

Lara blushed. 'I could stay in if you'd like, I feel bad going out just now . . . '

'Don't worry about me,' said Alex, managing a smile. 'I'm going to have a bath and an early night.'

Lara sighed. She really wished she hadn't agreed to go out with Mick now. Perhaps he wouldn't mind if she suggested Alex joined them? But even as she mulled over the possibility, she knew he would. And Alex was already turning on the bath water.

Lara went slowly downstairs, feeling oddly nervous. She poured herself a glass of wine and wondered what she would do if Mick cancelled again.

The very thought made her feel ill, and she had just taken a large gulp to calm herself when he came bouncing in. 'Sorry I'm late. That looks good, pour me a glass?'

Lara turned to reach for a glass from the cupboard, glad to have an excuse to look away from him. As ever he was rumpled and glowing with energy.

'Wouldn't you know it, I got caught by old McIntyre on my way out.'

'He wasn't complaining about you being late for your lesson, was he?' Lara had had a run in with their stickler of a headmaster over her own missed lesson the previous day and she knew all too well he didn't mince his words.

'No, thank goodness he didn't seem to know about that.' Mick took a sip of wine and smiled. 'Mmm, that's good.

He wanted to talk about the future of athletics in Dumfries and Galloway. I mean, at five-thirty on a Friday evening. Doesn't the man have a life?'

'That's why it's such a good school.' Although she had been mortified to be chastised by the Head, Lara had known it was only what she deserved, and part of her respected him for not letting it pass.

'Hmm. Give me five minutes to change and we can be off.'

'Alex's in the bathroom,' said Lara, feeling guilty once again for inflicting her friend on him.

'No problem, I had a shower at the school. I just need to change.' He gestured down at the mud splattered tracksuit, gave her another devastating grin, and bounded up the stairs two at a time.

* * *

Five minutes later Mick returned, attired now in jeans and a clean but crumpled T-shirt. Lara took this in with a quick glance. She didn't want to be seen staring. 'Right, where do you want to go?' he said. 'I'll need to drop Steve's car at his place and we can walk into town from there. Is that OK?'

'Fine,' said Lara, taking a last mouthful of wine. She must have drunk it too fast, she was feeling light-headed and shaky.

Mick put out an arm to usher her through the door before him. He barely touched her, but the warmth of his hand through her thin shirt made her heart give a little jolt.

The short journey passed in near silence. As they pulled up in the driveway of the shabby-grand house where Steve had his flat Mick said, 'I suppose we'd better go up and say hello.'

'That's fine by me.' Lara hadn't yet seen inside the flat and she was interested. Also, it would delay spending time alone with Mick.

Unlike Mick's house, this building had heaps of character, with curvy pillars flanking the front door, and old-fashioned green and maroon tiling in the hallway. 'It's lovely.'

'The flat needs masses of work doing,' said Mick as he led her up to the top floor.

'I know one or two places like that.'

'Yes, but you relish it, don't you?' Mick grinned at her and she realised she hadn't told him about work on Ladybank Row coming abruptly to a halt. She didn't want to think about that now. He rang the doorbell, and when they heard footsteps approaching he said quickly, 'Listen, we're not inviting him out with us. OK?'

'OK,' said Lara, turning slightly away so he wouldn't see her blush.

Steve asked briefly, but with clear affection, after Mick's father.

'He's out of danger thank goodness. I'll go over to see him again tomorrow, and then hopefully I can tail the visits off. I don't want them to start thinking they have a dutiful son or anything.'

'You should've kept the car, if you need it again in the morning.'

'Thought you might need it yourself. Right, we're off out for the evening. See you.'

As they walked along the road from Steve's place towards the town centre Mick took Lara's hand and linked his fingers through hers. 'Alone at last.'

Lara was looking around at the old houses, but all she could think about was his touch. She swung their two hands gently and felt happy.

They turned from Steve's side-street on to one of Loreburn's many main roads and immediately bumped into a group of youths. 'Hiya, Mick,' said one.

'Ooo, it's Miss Mason,' said another.

Lara tried to disentangle her fingers but Mick held on. 'Evening all,' he said, pushing his way easily through the crowd. 'Nice to see you.'

'Gee, Mr Jensen . . . '

'Oh, for some privacy,' said Mick grimly. 'We should have gone somewhere else. Anywhere else. There're no secrets in Loreburn.'

'I'd forgotten the down side of a small town.'

'Do you really mind?' he said, glancing sideways at her but keeping up the rapid pace, putting some distance between them and their pupils.

He looked so anxious she shook her head. 'Not really. It can't be helped in a place like this.'

'Too true. Which reminds me, how's Ryan getting on?'

'Ryan?' Lara realised she had forgotten all about the youth, who hadn't been seen since he phoned her the previous day. 'He was doing fine, but there's been a little hiccup. I'll tell you about it.'

Mick must have picked up on her serious tone for he paused to examine her, frowning now. 'Let's find somewhere to drink first.'

They were in the town centre now and he indicated a pub on their right, a noisy but spacious place where she had been once or twice before. 'Will this do?'

He held open the door for her and they found seats at a tiny corner table. After Mick had bought drink for them both Lara told him the tale of the asbestos. He listened carefully, which was another thing she liked about him. He could seem so light-hearted and easy going, but he knew when to be serious too.

'That isn't good,' he said.

'I know.' Lara frowned, all the pleasure she had felt earlier disappearing.

'I could put some feelers out about the builder who did the work,' offered Mick. 'I could check out if he's known for this kind of thing.'

'If it's no trouble, I'd appreciate it.'

'I'll ask Ed McAnulty. I know you don't like him but he has got his ear to the ground, he'll more than likely know whether this kind of thing goes on or not.'

Lara pulled a face. She'd rather not have anything to do with Ed McAnulty if she could help it.

'And now let's talk about something

a little more cheerful,' he said, touching her arm. 'Us.'

Lara found she liked it when he sat so close, but she couldn't help feeling self-conscious. Mick took her hand. 'It's good to get you on your own for once.'

'You see me at home.'

'But that's not the same, is it? There I'm your housemate. Here I could be . . . your boyfriend?'

Lara sat back and raised her glass for a sip, to make a barrier between them. 'But you're not my boyfriend, are you?'

'I want to be. Isn't that enough?' He reached over and took her hand again. He didn't have any of her hang-ups, and as he slowly stroked her fingers, she felt her doubts begin to slip away.

'It's just, I don't really . . . '

'You don't really?'

'Er.' She couldn't remember what she had been going to say. What was it? Ah, yes, the truth. 'I haven't really had many boyfriends. So I'm not used to . . . ' she gestured to the two of them, 'All this.'

He looked puzzled. 'I can't believe it. You're so beautiful.'

At that she blushed outright. He was so sweet — or was he joking? 'No I'm not. The reason I haven't had many boyfriends is . . . ' She took a deep breath. 'It's because the ones I like don't like me and the ones who like me aren't . . . ' She searched for the word. 'Worthwhile.'

He had taken her hand again and tangled his fingers with hers. He was still listening, but the smile had gone from his eyes. 'And where do I fit in?'

'You're different.'

'In what way?' He was listening. He really seemed to want to know. Or was that just another part of his charm?

'Because I, er, like you and you seem to like me back. At the same time.'

He smiled then, as though he had won a jackpot, and a little light seemed to sparkle in his eyes. 'That sounds good enough to me. We'll see how we get on from here, shall we?'

Lara knew it would be sensible to

argue, but somehow she didn't want to. She watched Mick as he made his way across the crowded room to get them another drink. She was paying this time but he insisted on going to the bar, saying she wasn't pushy enough to get served here. He received greetings from all sides, but kept on going, elbowing his way through the crowd. He wasn't aggressive, but he certainly knew how to get what he wanted. She wondered how many aspects of his life that applied to.

When Mick came back to the table with two glasses and a packet of crisps she said, 'How long have you worked at Loreburn High? You seem to know everyone there. And in here, for that matter.'

'Far too long,' said Mick lightly. 'But it's not a bad school, as you've probably gathered. A good head teacher makes a difference for pupils and staff alike.'

'That's true. We're very lucky in Mr McIntyre.' She twirled her glass in her fingers, musing. 'If you've been there so long, why haven't you gone for a promoted post?' She wondered why she hadn't asked him that when they had gone out for the meal. Probably because she had been too busy worrying about herself. Now she found she wanted to know more about him.

Mick said, 'There aren't any promoted posts going at the High. I would have to move elsewhere, or wait until Sandy retires, which won't be soon.'

'Have you looked elsewhere? There are two other secondary schools in Loreburn, aren't there?'

Mick pulled a face. 'Are you trying to get rid of me?'

'I just wondered. You are good at what you do, everyone says so.'

'Do they?' He sat up with mock pride. 'People talking nicely about me? They can't be feeling right.'

'Joke about it if you like, but you know it's true. The kids like you, you get a lot out of them and you put in goodness knows how many extra hours.'

'I do it because I enjoy it,' said Mick shortly.

'Why not reap the benefit? Go for promotion, the money's better and the hours couldn't be worse.'

'And the responsibility? Not to mention all the paperwork. No thanks.'

Lara wondered why she was pressing him. She wasn't at all keen on promotion for herself.

He put his head on one side and asked, 'Would I be better boyfriend material if I went for Head of Department?'

'Don't be silly.'

He grinned. 'I knew that would annoy you. But there are many who think that way.'

'I know.' She hesitated and then gave in. She found it was too tempting talking properly to him. 'I was acting Head of Department at my last school, and it was awful. Awful.'

'Why was that?'

So she told him. It wasn't acting as Head of Department that had been the problem, but what happened afterwards. She had thought she had done a good job, but when the new appointment was made, Miss Dunlop had done everything she could to undermine decisions Lara had made. She had turned the other staff against Lara and even reported her to the Headteacher for sloppy work.

'Sloppy work?' said Mick in amazement. 'You?'

'It's amazing how easy it is to make people look useless, if you try hard enough,' said Lara sadly.

'But not everyone thought you were useless. I know McIntyre had heard good things about you, that's why he was keen to have you down here.'

'I was lucky. My previous Head of Department put in a good word for me. He seemed to find my work satisfactory.'

'This Miss Dunlop sounds to have been totally out of order,' said Mick, looking annoyed now. 'Couldn't you have challenged her? Wouldn't the union have backed you?'

Lara shrugged. 'I'm not very good at confrontation. I decided it would be easiest if I just left. And so here I am.'

'And I'm very glad you are,' said Mick, touching her hand, but still frowning. 'But I hate to think of you being treated like that. Unfairness drives me mad.'

'It's over with now.' Lara found she was no longer hurt by the memories. Rather, she was warmed by Mick's concern. 'I just wanted to tell you so you would see I'm not one of those people who think promoted posts are the best thing in the world.'

'I'm glad to hear it.'

'Although I do think you would make a very good Head of Department . . .'

Mick just laughed and turned the subject to whether they should go to a Chinese or an Indian restaurant for a meal.

It Was My Fault

The following morning Lara rose early and was pleased to find Mick had already left to see his father. They had had a lovely evening, but she still wasn't sure where she stood with him. She was determined to devote her energies today to tracking down Gary Glover.

As it happened, this pursuit proved unnecessary. His dirty white van drew up at the house just after the two girls finished their breakfast. He climbed out and approached the door at what was for him a hurried pace.

'Well, well,' said Lara. 'What have we here?'

'I've just heard about your troubles,' he said as he entered, not waiting for their queries to begin. 'My wife's not been well and I was up at the hospital with her. Only got all your messages this morning.'

'I'm sorry about your wife,' said Alex.

'Yes,' agreed Lara. 'I hope she's all right? Now, do you think you can explain what's been going on at Ladybank Row? How did the asbestos land up in that river?'

'It wasn't me,' said the little man, shaking his sandy head. 'I'll have to check with the lads who took the load up to Lanarkshire for me, but I can't see why they'd dump it like that. We'd paid for disposal all right and proper. I'm sorry for your troubles.'

Lara frowned and Alex looked puzzled. They had expected the roofer to be guilty, or defensive, but instead he seemed genuinely concerned.

'So what happened? It doesn't make sense,' said Lara, adding hopefully, 'perhaps it wasn't our asbestos after all?'

'It's not like SEPA to make a mistake,' said Gary Glover gloomily. 'I'm off up to meet them now. I'll let you know what they say, but I can't make any sense of it.'

'Nor can we,' said Lara.

'Thanks for coming over,' said Alex. The poor man looked really worried. 'I hope your wife's better soon.'

'I think he was telling the truth,' she said, as soon as he was out of earshot.

'I suppose we'll just have to wait and see,' said Lara. Somehow, after the events of the last evening, she couldn't find it in herself to be too depressed about this. They would sort it out. 'Coffee?'

'No thanks. We've just had breakfast. I'm trying to cut down. Eat less and exercise more.'

Lara stared at her friend. 'I was only suggesting a coffee.'

'I know.' Alex smiled nervously. 'And you would manage to only have a drink. But every time I have a coffee I want a biscuit with it, and then another. So I've decided, I'm not going to eat or drink between meals. And I'm going to take more exercise. Like Mick.'

'That's, er, impressive.' Lara tried to see Alex in a tracksuit, jogging across town, and failed.

Alex blushed slightly. 'Maybe not exactly like Mick. But I'll try and walk more, at least.'

Lara wanted to hug her friend for making the decision, but was worried if she made too much of it she might put Alex off. So she merely smiled and said, 'Perhaps both of us could walk over to Ladybank Row later on. Even if we can't work on the houses we can still make plans, can't we? We should make a list of all the things that need doing.'

'Aren't you going to spend some time with Mick?'

'He's gone to see his dad,' said Lara quickly.

'You could have gone with him, couldn't you?'

'He invited me along, but I didn't want to go. I needed to be here, didn't I, to see Gary Glover?' Lara didn't tell Alex she really didn't want to meet Mick's family. Families made her nervous. She never felt at ease with her own and the brief trip to Dubai had made her realise she never would. She found it hard to understand other people's. Happy, bustling, affectionate ones, which she suspected Mick's would be, were the worst. 'So, are you willing to walk to Ladybank Row?'

Alex looked momentarily doubtful, and then, to Lara's delight, raised her rather plump chin and said, 'I am if you are.'

★ ★ ★

'I think I'll go back to England a week or so earlier than we had originally planned.' Elizabeth broke this news to Derek over breakfast. He was a morning person and she hoped he could be more amenable to agreeing with her at this hour.

She had been thinking over this possibility ever since Lara's departure, and now she had reached a decision.

She waited nervously as Derek poured himself a second cup of coffee.

'A week earlier? Why would you want to do that?'

'I'll have everything packed here by next weekend, and all my goodbyes will have been said.'

'I still have to work until the following Friday. It's in my contract.'

'But you could manage without me, couldn't you?'

'But why would you want to go over early?' Derek didn't seem annoyed, just interested. In the bright morning sunlight his white hair shone brightly, but his face looked tired. Elizabeth felt a pang. He needed her. Was she doing the wrong thing leaving him alone for that last week? But then she remembered Lara. She had to do this.

'I want to spend some time with Lara.' There, she had said it. 'I want to see these funny little houses she and Alex have bought, and meet her housemate. And just, well, see what her life is like these days.' Her voice trailed off. She didn't expect Derek to understand. He had never been close to his daughter. It didn't seem to worry him, but it worried her. If he tried to persuade her to change her mind she was still going to go. She was!

'That's not a bad idea,' he said musingly, patting his lips with a napkin. 'I don't know why she thinks we don't take an interest in her. Of course we do. We're just not the sort of parents who interfere in their child's life.'

'I don't want to interfere. I just want to — see.'

'If that's what you want, then do it. I'm sure the travel agent can change your flights. But don't take on too much, will you? Travelling to Scotland will be quite tiring enough, don't let Lara talk you into doing any of the work for her. You'll need to save your energies for sorting out the house in Devon.'

'I won't do too much,' said Elizabeth. She couldn't believe how well this was going. She had already spoken to the travel agent and knew she could change her flights.

'Maybe whilst you're there you can

make her see sense,' mused Derek. 'Didn't she say there was a builder interested in buying the derelict houses off them? Now if you could persuade her to accept his offer and buy herself a nice modern place I'd be very pleased.'

'I'll see what I can do,' said Elizabeth. She had no intention of trying to persuade Lara into anything. Yes, it would have been wonderful if their daughter had wanted to move to Devon. But she hadn't. It was just important Lara was happy, wherever she was. And that Elizabeth should see her. She still remembered Lara's words, on that last evening of her visit. Don't worry, you probably won't see me again for years. It was as if she thought her parents didn't want to see her. Elizabeth was determined to show her how wrong she was.

* * *

For Lara, the next few days passed in a haze — a happy one. As long as she didn't think about families, and Mick didn't press her about them, she could relax. She was discovering that spending time with Mick was just incredibly good fun.

When the new school week started she realised with a jolt that it was less than a month until the summer holidays. It was hard to believe how much time had passed already. She always enjoyed the long summer break, and this year she had so much more to look forward to. Surely, surely they would be able to start work on the houses again soon, and with weeks of free time on her hands they would really make progress on the houses.

And, perhaps, she would spend even more time with Mick. She pushed that thought quickly aside. No point in having unrealistic expectations.

On Tuesday Mr McIntyre popped into her classroom as the bell went for the lunchtime break. This was the second time he had sought her out in the last couple of weeks. The first had been that uncomfortable conversation about her missed lesson, and she hoped he hadn't come to discuss that again.

He leant casually against one of the desks and she waited for the explosion. 'How have you found your first few months in Loreburn?' he asked instead.

'Er, fine,' she said, doubtfully.

'Excellent.'

Lara added, 'I hope everything is all right from your point of view? The way I'm teaching the syllabus and so on? I'm really sorry about missing that lesson, it was a one-off, it won't happen again.'

He smiled at her. 'I'm sure it won't. I've had excellent reports from Mark Frazer and seen nothing but good myself. You are definitely an asset to the school.'

'Thank you.' Lara blushed. She had never been praised by her other Headteachers. Perhaps he was building up to some bad news? That was the most likely thing. He was probably just softening her up first. She said quickly,

'I think I've settled in now. I'm starting to understand how things work here. It takes time but hopefully I'm nearly there.'

'I'm sure you are,' he said with a small smile. 'More 'nearly there' than half the teachers who have been with us for years, but that's not what I wanted to discuss with you. I don't know whether it has come to your ears yet, but Mark is considering taking early retirement. If he does go there'll be a Head of Department vacancy in August. I think you should consider applying.'

Lara was speechless. She felt briefly a warm satisfaction in his approval, and then horror at what he was suggesting.

'I'm not really sure . . . '

'Think about it,' he continued blandly. 'Your classes are admirably organised. You get on well with staff and children alike. That trip to the Bass Rock was a great success and Mark assures me it was entirely down to you.'

'That's very kind of him,' said Lara faintly. Sometimes you actually didn't want credit to be given where credit was due. 'I'm not really looking for promotion . . . '

'You don't need to decide anything now. There isn't a definite vacancy yet, but I thought it wouldn't do any harm for you to mull the idea over.' He paused and examined her with raised eyebrows. 'You wouldn't want yourself to be influenced by other people's attitudes to extra responsibility, would you?'

He left her without waiting for a reply. She was pretty sure who he was referring to. Mick. And she felt defensive on Mick's behalf. Who said he didn't want extra responsibility? He took on enough in his own way.

The more Lara thought about this conversation the more it worried her. She didn't want this choice to be thrust upon her. She had decided against ever going for a Head of Department post again, and she was happy with that decision. Unfortunately, from what she had heard, Mr McIntyre wasn't good at taking no for an answer. She sighed heavily. Why did life have to be so complicated?

★　★　★

'Be careful you don't hurt Lara,' said Steve.

'I'm not going to hurt her.' Mick stared at him. Where had this come from? They had retired to the pub after Friday evening football practice. He would have gone home if Lara had been there, but she and Alex had gone to see a film.

'You always say that. But when the romance wears off . . .'

'This is different.'

Steve raised one dark eyebrow disbelievingly. 'Well, it's nothing to do with me, I suppose.'

'Exactly.'

'But she's a nice lassie, not your normal type.'

'Leave it,' said Mick. It wasn't like Steve to launch into a heart to heart.

He preferred the usual Steve.

'Let her down gently, OK?'

'I'm not intending to let her down at all,' said Mick, and then felt a tiny shadow of doubt. What exactly did he mean by that? He wasn't intending to let her down, but he wasn't quite sure what it was he intended.

He certainly had no desire to change the way things were with Lara at the moment. The last fortnight had been, well, pretty good. Why did Steve of all people have to introduce such a serious note?

Steve seemed to feel he had said enough and reached for his pint on the wooden table. They were sitting out in the garden in very un-Loreburn-like sunshine.

'I envy you your job at times like this,' he said. 'Summer holidays on the horizon. Two whole months with nothing to do.'

'Seven weeks, actually,' said Mick, but grinned all the same. There were some very good things about being a teacher.

'What're you going to do with yourself? You'll soon get bored.'

'I can see I'll be spending a fair amount of time at Ladybank Row. Always assuming they get permission to start work again, which they're hoping for this week. And I've got this youth football tournament happening in the first week. I don't know why I thought it would be a good idea.'

Steve frowned. 'I don't understand what SEPA are playing at. It's not the girls' fault if their contractor disposed of the asbestos illegally, is it?'

Mick didn't understand it either. 'Something's not right. They seem to think the roofer guy is honest too, yet the asbestos was definitely there.'

'There're dodgy dealings all through the building trade,' said Steve, who would certainly know. 'Now, if my brother was involved then I wouldn't be one bit surprised . . . '

Mick felt a flicker of concern. Why should the mention of Ed worry him? He and Steve usually kept firmly off that topic of his brother. Ed had not invited Mick for a drink a second time and he was happy to leave things.

'Why should it have anything to do with your brother?' he said.

'I'm not saying it has. Ed's always very careful to keep his nose clean. But it's surprising how many of his competitors have been caught out by this regulation or that. It makes you wonder, doesn't it?'

Mick's unease grew. 'You're not saying Ed would set them up . . . ?'

'Not necessarily. Although I'm sure he'd have no qualms about reporting people to the powers that be. Still, how would he know about what was going on at Ladybank Row? He wouldn't even know they were having the asbestos removed.'

Mick said nothing. Ed did know the girls were having the asbestos removed, because Mick had told him so himself. He needed to think this over and then, very possibly, he needed to go and see Ed McAnulty. How could he, Mick Jensen, have been so naïve?

It was early Saturday evening and Lara was preparing chicken pesto. She presumed Mick would be back to eat with them. The thought made her smile. He had begun to eat with them most evenings, contributing generous amounts of food and wine, and sharing the washing up. This relationship was still such a precious new thing she didn't dare look to the future to see where it might go, but it felt unbelievably good.

Mick wasn't like any boyfriend she had had before. He was very attractive but he was also funny, and good. It was a strange word to use but she was sure it was the right one. He was a good man and with that, for the moment, she was content.

He returned half an hour or so later. Alex was still in the bath and Lara had just finished making the salad.

'Hi there,' she said cheerfully. 'I wondered if you'd be back for food. I've just done pasta with chicken and pesto and . . . Is something wrong?'

Mick had stopped in the kitchen doorway and was regarding her with a fixed, almost angry expression. 'I've just been to see Ed McAnulty. And now I know the answer to the mystery of the asbestos.' The green eyes flashed with fury. 'It was my fault.'

'Wha-at?'

'I suppose I should say it was Ed's fault, certainly his doing. But if I hadn't let him know about the asbestos then he couldn't have done what he did.'

Lara had never seen Mick so angry. In fact, she had rarely seen him cross at all, which was one of the things she so liked about him. Now he seemed to be in a simmering rage, fists clenched and mouth grim.

'Come and sit down,' she said warily. 'And tell me what's going on.' If he sat down he wouldn't look so intimidating.

She pushed a can of soft drink into his hand but he put it down on the table with a bang. 'It was my fault! I can't tell you how sorry I am.'

'Perhaps first you can explain what you're talking about?'

Mick groaned and then, at last, sat down. He cracked open the can, glared at if for a moment, and then took a drink. 'It was Ed's doing, the whole asbestos fiasco. He arranged for someone — I'm not sure who — to take some of the stuff from Ladybank Row and dump it in the river. Then he drew it to the attention of the farmer who reported you to SEPA. He's denying it all, of course, but it's as clear as the hand before your eyes.'

'But why . . . ?'

'To get back at you. Maybe to delay you so you'd run out of money or enthusiasm and sell the properties to him. Ed doesn't like not getting his own way.'

Lara thought of Ed's brooding anger and could well believe that. 'It won't work with us,' she said, but she bit her lip. The fear of a hefty fine had been hanging over them. How easy would it have been to continue if that had happened? How could someone do this to them?

'No, but it might have done, mightn't it? It's wasted weeks of your time and got you into an awful lot of trouble.'

'Not now,' said Lara slowly. 'Not if we can show them McAnulty is to blame.'

'Knowing and proving are two separate things. But I can think of one or two ways we might do it.'

Lara smelt something from the stove behind her and swung around to grab the pan. 'Nearly burnt it.' She turned the ring off and put the food to one side. She couldn't think about that now.

'I'm really sorry,' said Mick, still glaring at his drink. 'If I hadn't happened to mention the asbestos to Ed he would never have been able to do this.'

'I think he knew about the asbestos already,' said Lara slowly. 'Remember, he'd had a good look at the houses himself.'

'Well, he wouldn't have known when you were having it removed, or who by. He just asked me one or two questions and I gave the whole thing away. And there was I, so pleased to be able to show him how well you were doing.'

'I'm sure it's not your fault,' said Lara. She hated to see him so miserable. 'And at least you've got to the bottom of it. Maybe we'll be able to start work again now, which would be brilliant. Come on, let's eat. We can think about what to do afterwards.'

'I need to speak to Gary Glover myself, and maybe Steve. No, on second thoughts, not Steve. And tomorrow we get on to SEPA. And possibly the police.'

Lara didn't like the sound of the police. 'We'll talk about it later. Right, come on, let's eat.' Lara went to call Alex and then served the overcooked pasta. She should have been relieved the mystery of the asbestos had been solved, but instead she felt more anxious than ever. It was horrible to think someone had purposely set out to hurt them. It reminded her all over again that there were some unpleasant people in this world, even here in Loreburn.

And throughout the evening Mick glowered at her between the phone calls he insisted on making. It was almost as if by blaming himself he was putting up a barrier between them.

Lara's Mother Meets Mick

Despite Mick's suspicions and numerous phone calls, the girls still did not have permission to restart work at Ladybank Row. Ed McAnulty categorically denied any involvement with the asbestos and SEPA insisted on having proof. For the first couple of days Lara had accepted that Mick might sort it all out. She was nervous of Ed, and not keen to approach him herself.

However, by the end of school on the Tuesday afternoon she had had enough of the waiting. She prowled around Mick's house, trying to shake off her gloom, trying to think of a way forward. It had been a miserable day with dark clouds low in the sky and a vicious wind whipping around corners. Her classes had been fractious which had done nothing to improve her mood.

With a huff of annoyance she pulled

on a jacket and went out to find Alex in the back garden. The garden here was nothing like those at Ladybank Row. It was tiny, with a weed-infested patio and a small lawn that was more moss than grass. Alex had decided to turn her attentions here whilst they were being kept away from Ladybank Row. Mick had given her free rein to do whatever she wanted.

'How're you getting on?' said Lara, pulling her coat more closely around her.

Alex's long hair was, unusually, hanging loose and the wind was beating it into her face. She pushed it back with one arm as she looked up and smiled. She smiled so much more often these days. 'Fine.'

'What are you doing?'

Alex had a spade in her hand and had marked out an area at the end of the lawn with pegs and string. 'I'm putting in a flower bed.'

'Oh,' said Lara doubtfully. 'Will Mick be any good at looking after a flower bed?'

Alex gave a very faint smile. 'I'll plant shrubs in it. Low maintenance, you know.'

'That's good.' Lara had the impression Mick used the lawn for nothing other than the occasional football practice. Hopefully the shrubs would be hardy. 'I'm sorry you're having to waste your time here. You were getting on so well at the Row.'

'It's OK. And Mick seems pleased. I'm glad to do him a favour for a change.'

Lara nodded approvingly, but she couldn't help her thoughts turning back to Ed. 'This is ridiculous,' she said suddenly. 'I'm not going to let him bully us.'

'Who?' said Alex, confused.

'There must be something we can do, some connection we can make,' said Lara, thinking hard how. If someone else had been into Ladybank Row, surely they would have left a tiny bit of evidence? Wouldn't she and the others have noticed? And then she realised she had. That time when the door had not been locked properly and everyone had denied responsibility. That had to be it! Whoever had access to the keys was the link.

'I'll see you later,' said Lara, and turned on her heel.

Why hadn't she thought of this before? Clearly the only thing to do was to go and see Ed McAnulty face to face. Now she had something to challenge him with, he'd have to admit it. She suppressed a little quiver of doubt and jumped into her car. She would do it now, before she lost her nerve.

Luckily she knew where to go. Mick had once pointed out the McAnulty house to her, a sprawling detached building on the edge of town. Ed ran his business from an office in what used to be the double garage. It had a huge sign, *McAnulty and Sons, Building Contractors*, and a couple of vans out the front. It gave an intimidating impression of prosperity.

Lara parked her little car on the gravel beside one of the vans and gripped her hands together, willing herself to go through with this. She felt that same dull panic she had known when Miss Dunlop had accused her, wrongly, of destroying the Department, and she hadn't known how to fight back. This time she was going to.

Ed McAnulty was in the wrong. She had had enough of people treating her unfairly and getting away with it. As she climbed out of the car the sun appeared from behind the flowering clouds, turning the lower part of the sky and all her surroundings golden. Maybe it was a sign.

Even so, Lara nearly lost her nerve when a girl at the reception desk told her Mr McAnulty was out. She could wait if she wanted but the girl didn't know when he would be back. It was the perfect opportunity to run away and consider whether this was really such a good idea.

Then they heard a car draw up

outside and the girl said, glancing out, 'That'll be him now.' She sounded bored and when Ed appeared in the doorway she didn't even brother to introduce Lara. Not that she needed any introduction.

Her mouth went dry when she saw Ed. He was dressed, most unexpectedly, in a dark suit and tie. This made his massive size all the more impressive and the scowl he gave when he saw her did nothing to put her at ease.

'What are you doing here?'

'I came to see you. Perhaps I can have a word?'

'Now you'd like a word, would you? You didn't want to talk to me when I wanted to discuss things.'

The receptionist looked up, interested. Ed glared at her. He indicated a door to Lara. 'Come on. We can talk in here.'

The office was a surprise. There was a big, showy desk which Lara might have expected, but the plain white walls and two beautiful paintings indicated another side to Ed McAnulty. She felt wrong-footed. She had come here to challenge him, to point out what an ignorant person he was. Despite what everyone said, she hadn't really thought of him as a successful businessman.

'If you've come to tell me you're ready to sell, then I'll be happy to speak to you.' Ed towered over her, dark eyebrows meeting in a fierce scowl. 'Otherwise you're wasting your time.'

Why did everyone think they could decide whether she was wasting her time or not? Why did they all think they knew best? Lara had had enough.

She put her hands on her hips and stood to the maximum of her not very great height. 'I think, Mr McAnulty, you might want to be careful about the way you speak to me. Threatening another person is punishable in a court of law. I've had enough of your posturing. I've had enough of your pretending to put in an offer and then backing out. And I've had absolutely enough of your planting asbestos where it was never left by our contractors and reporting us to SEPA. We're not putting up with this any more.'

'Having a little difficulty with SEPA, are you?'

'You know very well we are. And we know why, too.'

'Mick Jensen has already mentioned it. I don't know why he thinks it has anything to do with me.' He smiled, not amused.

The smile was the last straw. Lara was suddenly too furious to be afraid. 'Mick thinks this had something to do with you because you were asking him what was going on at Ladybank Row.'

'Just showing a little professional interest.'

'And I think it has something to do with you because I know someone was in the houses a few days before all this happened. Someone who shouldn't have been there.'

From the slight stiffening in Ed's demeanour she felt she was on the right track. 'You got a key from somewhere, didn't you? And you or someone on your behalf was scouting round the houses. I know you threatened me and I'll find out how you got that key and then I'll have some real evidence for the police.'

'Now, now, why would we want to involve the police?'

'Don't you realise the trouble you've caused us? I could get the police in right now. We're facing a massive fine. Or should I say you are? And what about our reputation?'

'You don't have a reputation,' he said with a smirk. 'Not any more.'

'And nor will you, if this gets out.' Lara stood her ground, even when he jutted his chin out threateningly. 'You can't do this,' she said. 'I won't let you get away with it.'

'Going to set Mick and my little brother, Steve, on to me? Now that I'd like to see.'

'We don't need to use force against you. We've got brains. I know everyone who has had access to keys. I'll check them all out and when one of them leads back to you then I'll contact the police. Is that what you want?'

'I think you're making a bit too many assumptions there.' Ed's tone was still belligerent but his expression was shifty and Lara felt more than ever she was on to something. She racked her brains. She and Alex both had keys. Ryan O'Donnell hadn't been given one but it was possible he could have got hold of one of theirs. She hoped not, for Mick's sake. And then there was Gary Glover. Lara trusted him, but that didn't mean she trusted his employees. Yes, that might be the place to start.

'I think I might go and have a little chat with Gary Glover,' she said. 'See which of his men have been working on site and what they might be able to tell us.'

'Now, now, you don't need to do that,' said Ed. Bingo. That was it. 'You don't want to be too hasty. It might all have been an, er, a little misunderstanding, mightn't it?'

'You're evil,' said Lara, staring at

him. She hadn't really expected him to admit it. 'You set us up. How could you?'

'I'm not saying I did, but why don't you let me have a word with one or two people, see if I can sort things out for you. Wouldn't want any bad feeling, would we? You are a friend of my brother's, after all.'

Lara hesitated. Ed deserved to be dragged through the courts, but if he could put things right for them, quickly, without that, maybe it was for the best?

'I'll give you twenty-four hours,' she said, in what she hoped was an intimidating tone.

* * *

When she got back to Mick's house she found she was shaking. She couldn't believe what she had just done, and nor could the others.

'You went there on your own?' demanded Mick.

'You were really brave,' said Alex.

'Why didn't you wait for me?' asked Mick. 'It was my fault all this happened. I should have been there to sort it out.'

'It wasn't your fault. It was Ed's fault. And why shouldn't I go on my own? Don't you think I'm capable?'

Mick opened his mouth and then closed it again. He clearly did think she was useless. Well, she had shown them. Lara felt more proud of herself than she had in months. It was a very good feeling.

Nobody was quite sure what Ed McAnulty did to resolve things, but they had permission to resume work on Ladybank Row by the end of that week. One good thing had come of that long delay: Lara had been able to line up no end of people to start work immediately permission was given. From the following Monday they had workmen in the house every day, checking the plumbing and replacing the electrics, in addition to Gary Glover's men doing the roof. Life was back on track.

*   *   *

Lara frowned at the knock on the front door. She was just about to leave for Ladybank Row and wasn't expecting anyone. Mick was out and Alex had disappeared off on her own, as she had taken to doing surprisingly often these days. With a sigh, Lara went to open the door.

'Mum!' This was the very last person she expected to see here in Loreburn. Her mother should still be in Dubai!

'Hello, darling.' Her mother, beautifully groomed as always, leant in to kiss her cheek. 'How are you?'

'Is everything all right? Why are you here?' Lara couldn't get her head around this sudden arrival. Her mother never did anything unexpected.

'Everything is fine. We were all packed up and ready to leave Dubai, so I thought, why don't I come over early and spend a little time with you.' She smiled, but Lara thought she saw a hint of nervousness.

She was about to say, But why? then she changed it to, 'Gosh.' She took a breath. 'Goodness. Well. Would you like to come in?'

'I'd love to. I'll just need a moment to pay off the taxi. I asked him to wait in case you weren't in. I wasn't sure . . .'

Lara could think of all manner of things her mother wouldn't be sure about. How had this happened, her mother arriving unannounced on her doorstep? She was stunned.

All the same, she couldn't help smiling. She slipped on some sandals and went out to help her mother with her luggage.

'Of course, I'm not expecting to stay here with you, you won't have room. Perhaps you can recommend a nice hotel and take me over there in a little while? I don't want to be in your way.'

'I'm sure we can sort something out. Come on in.' Lara led the way into the narrow hall. 'That's the sitting room, this is the kitchen. Shall we have a cup

225

of tea — or would you prefer coffee?'
Lara was aware she was now chattering
too much because she was nervous. She
knew her mother would be thinking
how scruffy, not to mention untidy, the
house was. At least her father wasn't
here to see it, he would have been truly
appalled. 'There's not much to see here,'
she said, gesturing vaguely with her hand.

'It's, er, very nice and compact,' said
her mother diplomatically.

When Lara had made the tea and
carried the tray through to the sitting
room, her mother said more warmly,
'Now, this is nice. Lovely colours.'

Lara was surprised and pleased. Her
throws and pretty cushions had trans-
formed the room into quite a haven,
but her parents' houses were always so
pale and tasteful, she hadn't expected
approval.

They chatted a little about the
weather, and her mother's journey.
Then Lara asked the question she had
wanted to ask since her mother's
appearance.

'Mum, why didn't you tell me you were coming? I could have met you at the station, or even at the airport. I could have made sure there was a room booked in a hotel.'

Her mother touched her neat, short hair nervously. 'I wasn't sure you would want to see me,' she said, in little more than a whisper.

'But of course ... ' Lara began to protest, and then tailed off. She remembered how hurt she had been when she left Dubai. How their disapproval had rankled. She wasn't sure how she would have felt if her father had turned up unannounced, but her mother was different. Especially when she had taken the risk of making this visit. 'Of course I want to see you,' she said, the words choking in her throat. 'How could you think otherwise?'

'I'm so glad,' said her mother, smiling properly for the first time. 'We can have such fun. I'll stay for a week if you can put up with me that long. I won't get in your way, I know you have to work. But it would mean so much to me to meet your friends, see something of your life.'

'It'll be a pleasure,' said Lara. To her surprise, she found she meant it.

★   ★   ★

Lara hadn't realised what fun it could be having her mother around. She didn't remember her mother being so light-hearted, but maybe that was because her father wasn't there too. He was always so serious. Now they could giggle together over Alex's little accident with the wheelbarrow, spend ages wandering around the supermarket debating what to cook for supper, sit out in Mick's tidied-up garden and chatter over a glass of white wine.

It was coming to the end of the school year and Lara could feel herself relaxing. Having her mother here just made it seem all the more like a holiday.

The only downside was that Mick

wanted to join in, and Lara thought it would be best if she kept him and her mother apart. Why would he want to get to know her family? She tried to show that she didn't expect him to spend time with them, but it was difficult without being rude.

Her mother announced her intention of taking Lara and Alex out for a meal on the last evening. Lara was pleased Alex and her mum were getting on, they had never seemed to take to each other before, and was delighted when Alex accepted the invitation. Mrs Mason had opted for the restaurant in the rather smart hotel where she was staying, and both girls were eager to try it. It had a good reputation but was outside their normal price bracket.

'I was wondering if I should invite your landlord, too,' she said, as she and the two girls sat in the garden in the late evening sunshine.

For a moment Lara couldn't think who her mother meant. She rarely thought of Mick as her 'landlord'. 'I'm sure that's not necessary . . . '

'He has been very helpful. Even offering to move out of his own room to let me stay here, which was out of the question of course, but a nice thought.' She lowered her voice. 'And although he looks rather young, he's quite sensible underneath it all, isn't he?'

'He's great,' said Alex, to Lara's astonishment. 'He's one of the world's good guys. Did I tell you he has persuaded Ryan to come back and work for us? Poor boy, he got quite a fright when that inspector came round, but he's back on the job today and proving very useful. Mick says it'll do him good, too, keep him out of trouble.'

'Was that the disreputable young man I saw filling the skip?' said Lara's mother, sounding less enthusiastic. 'I'm glad you found him useful. I have to say, I couldn't understand a word he said.' Lara hoped the mention of Ryan might have made her mother cool towards the idea of inviting Mick to join them for a meal, but it wasn't to be.

When he returned after his Friday evening football practice she immediately invited him along and he, of course, accepted with alacrity.

Perhaps this would be a good thing? Then Mick could see what her mother was really like, and realise how unsuited Lara and he were.

* * *

Mick made an effort with his appearance for the meal. He didn't take much trouble over his everyday clothes, because they didn't matter to him, but if he needed to be smart he could be. Alex had also made an effort and Lara realised with a jolt that her friend must have been serious about her desire to lose weight. She certainly looked different, not thin exactly but pretty in the soft floaty dress and with her long hair pinned up.

Lara felt as though she was the one who hadn't taken enough trouble. She was wearing a sleeveless linen dress she had worn more than once before and there wasn't much she could do with her short hair. She shrugged at her own concern. What was she worrying about? It was just a meal with family and friends, nothing special.

The restaurant was very different to the one she had visited with Mick. Here everything was traditional, waiters clad in black and white and tables set with an intimidating array of cutlery and glasses.

'This is posh,' said Alex with a nervous giggle.

'It's meant to be,' said Mick, seeming as at ease here as on the playing fields. 'It's always had the reputation as the smart place in Loreburn. The prices certainly make sure the riff raff don't flood through the doors.'

'Have you been here before?' asked Lara, surprised.

'A couple of times. Once for my parents' Silver Wedding anniversary and once for some other occasion, I forget what.'

As they took their seats at the table, Lara's mother began to ask him about his family and Lara could have groaned when she saw how well the two of them were getting on. Mick was a little flippant as usual, but his love for his family was clear and Elizabeth seemed to be lapping it up. This is not going to plan at all.

'Did you ever come here with your gran?' Lara asked Alex, hoping to change the subject.

Alex shook her head slowly. 'No, Gran didn't like eating out. Don't you remember how she liked things the traditional way, a proper tea at five in the afternoon, with a teapot in its cosy on the table?' She smiled gently as she remembered, for once not looking pained by her loss.

Lara smiled too. She remembered one of her last visits to Alex's gran, when she and Alex were already working and had taken along a bottle of wine as they would have done to friends. Alex's gran hadn't quite known what to do with it, and compromised by serving cups of tea and glasses of wine simultaneously with the late afternoon meal. It had made for a very odd mixture.

'Your gran was great,' she said.

'She sounds lovely,' agreed her mother. 'We were very grateful to her for inviting Lara for holidays when she couldn't make it back to the Middle East.'

'We loved having her,' said Alex easily. 'Although Gran always thought it was such a shame for you, to see so little of her.'

Lara cringed. That was not the right thing to say to her mother. Despite the effort Elizabeth was making now, Lara didn't believe either of her parents had really regretted not seeing her during those holidays. If they had, they could have come over to the UK, couldn't they?

'We're going to make up for that now,' said her mother, smiling tremulously. 'Devon isn't as close as I'd like but it'll be much easier than visiting from Dubai. And once Derek has retired he'll have time on his hands, I'm sure he'll be happy to explore Scotland.'

Lara made a doubtful noise, but didn't actually disagree.

'I've never been to Devon,' said Mick, seemingly unaware of her tension. 'Ridiculous, isn't it, when it's relatively close? Our holidays always seemed to be elsewhere in Scotland or, if we wanted sun, in Spain.'

'You'll have to come and visit us once we've settled in,' said Elizabeth. 'We'll get Lara to bring you down.'

Lara stared at her mother. The worst thing was, she actually seemed to mean it.

It was during their second course that Lara started to notice what Alex was eating. She had had a tiny prawn starter for her first course, and was now eating grilled trout and salad. No chips. No bread rolls.

'You don't think you're taking this

dieting thing too seriously, do you?' she said, beginning to be alarmed. This was so unlike Alex, who loved her food. Lara realised that for the last few weeks Alex had rarely eaten with her, always having some reason to be away at meal times.

Alex blushed as the others turned to look at her. 'I'm fine.'

'Losing some weight isn't a bad thing, but you don't want to take it too far,' said Lara.

'I won't take it too far. I'm following something called Diane's Diet plan.'

'Who on earth is Diane?'

'I've heard about that,' said Mick. 'One of the female PE teachers is doing it. Don't you have to attend group sessions and all sorts of things?'

Alex blushed even more. 'That's right. I saw it advertised in the paper and I thought — why not? I didn't think I'd manage to stick to it on my own but the group are really nice.'

Lara shook her head in amazement. So that was where Alex had been going when she disappeared on her own.

'Why didn't you say?'

Alex shrugged and said softly, 'I was worried I might not stick to it and you would be disappointed in me . . .'

'Oh Alex.' Lara leaned across to hug her, quite overwhelmed. 'How could you think that? I could never be disappointed in you.'

'You do set very high standards, Lara,' said her mother, considering her with her head on one side. 'You probably don't realise it, but you do. You're very like your father.'

Lara looked at her in horror. She was not a work-obsessed perfectionist. She was not!

'That's why everything you do, you do so well,' said Mick, as though this was something to be cheerful about. 'It's that serious level of application you have. I don't know anyone as serious as you.'

'Rubbish,' said Lara, looking desperately to Alex for support.

'It's true,' said Alex gently. 'Sometimes it's hard to live up to your standards. But look where it gets you. Ladybank Row is going to be brilliant.'

'And one of these days, you'll probably end up as Head of Department,' added Mick, not sounding quite so cheerful.

'Oh darling, that would be wonderful,' said her mother.

Lara took a sip of wine that she had trouble swallowing, and determinedly changed the subject. They were quite wrong, but it didn't seem she was going to be able to change their opinions.

Lara Breaks Mick's Heart

Lara wished she wasn't such a fool. She had known getting involved with Mick was a bad idea, and it clearly was, look how he had sided with her mother against her.

They were just having a bit of fun, a light-hearted relationship, but that wasn't her way. She knew, now, that it wasn't her way. Her other relationships hadn't worked out because she hadn't cared enough. Maybe she had even chosen the men in question because she knew she would never care enough.

With Mick it was different. With Mick she was afraid she could care too much, which made her want to run. He was interested in her now, but he wasn't the sort to settle down, he had never intimated he was looking for a long-term relationship. Hadn't he said he wasn't serious like her? She gave a little shrug as she thought of his words. Fool that she was.

Men like Mick were not for her. She should never have allowed herself to get involved, or at least have ended it after a few dates, but her courage had failed her. Strange. She was usually good at ending things.

★ ★ ★

Over the meal that evening Mick said, 'Did you hear that Mark Frazer is retiring? Sandy Woods told me this afternoon. Bit of a surprise, I thought he was one of those who would stay until he dropped.'

Lara turned. 'So it's definite, then?' Then she caught the expression on Mick's face and wished she had held her tongue. Mr McIntyre had asked her not to mention Mark's possible retirement to anyone and she had been more than happy to keep quiet about it. 'I mean, is he really?'

'You knew, didn't you?' Mick frowned.

'But you didn't think to tell me.'

'It wasn't definite so I couldn't say anything.'

Mick's friendly tone was suddenly gone. For a reason Lara couldn't fathom he seemed put out.

'So you're thinking of going for the job yourself, are you? Goodness. Sandy implied as much, but I said you wouldn't be interested.'

Lara shrugged uneasily. 'Mr McIntyre mentioned something a while ago but . . . '

'He wants you to go for the promotion? No wonder you don't want to get into his bad books. Always the good girl, aren't you?'

'Mick, what's the problem? I'm sorry I didn't mention Mark leaving, but I didn't think it was a big thing. And whether I go for promotion or not is up to me, isn't it?' Her heart sank as she said the words.

She'd told Mr McIntyre she wasn't interested and that was the truth, but now Mick seemed to be holding it against her and it was really nothing to do with him. She would make up her own mind.

'Yes, of course, it's up to you,' said Mick, putting down his mug with a bang. 'Just like everything else in your life. I think I'll go out and see Steve.' He strode out the front door without another word.

* * *

Lara headed over to Ladybank Row straight after school. Normally she worked much later, but it was the last week of term and even she couldn't find much to do in the way of marking or preparation. She didn't want to go home and face Mick, who was still being very aloof. So Ladybank Row it was.

As ever, her spirits lifted as she turned into the little cul-de-sac. She had thought she might tire of the funny little houses and all the hard work they entailed, but so far she hadn't. She loved them as much as ever. For themselves and for the good influence they were having on Alex.

It was wonderful to see her friend escaping the depression. It wasn't just the weight loss, it was the liveliness that had returned to her expression, the genuine bounce in her step.

Lara wandered in through the open door of Number One calling, 'Coo-ee, it's me. Where are you Alex? A-lex!'

'Upstairs. Come and see.'

The cheery tone of Alex's voice made Lara smile all the more. She took the stairs two at a time and joined her friend in the large front bedroom.

'Wow!' The plasterers had been and instead of tatty, uneven walls there was now an expanse of smooth grey. The joiner had fitted new windows the previous week and it was really starting to look like a proper house.

'This is brilliant.'

'Isn't it? They did all the upstairs rooms today. And wait till you see the bathroom. The new bath has been fitted and . . . '

Alex paused as they both listened. A vehicle was drawing up outside. They frowned at each other.

'Who can that be?' said Lara. 'Are we expecting anyone?'

'Not as far as I know.'

They heard the heavy footsteps of a man approaching the house.

'Better go and see,' said Lara, feeling unaccountably nervous.

She was right to be nervous. Their visitor was none other than Ed McAnulty. She had bested him in their last encounter, but she was still wary of him.

'What do you want?' she said.

Alex shot her a disapproving look. Their school had put a lot of emphasis on good manners. 'Hello, there. Can we help you?'

Ed stuck out a large hand. 'I'm Ed McAnulty. How do you do? I don't think we've ever been introduced, but I presume you are Alex? Lara I know, of course.'

Lara stayed a step behind Alex,

studying the man suspiciously. He wore jeans and a rugby jersey and was not so intimidating as in his suit, but he was still very large.

'Pleased to meet you,' said Alex politely.

The man took a deep breath and Lara prepared herself for bad news, or another threat. He said, 'I've come to apologise. Causing you problems with the asbestos was absolutely wrong of me, I don't know what I was thinking of.'

'Making a profit for yourself?' said Lara, glaring.

The man's expression darkened but he continued. 'I hope everything has been sorted out now? I know you've been making progress, having plasterers here and so on.'

Lara supposed she shouldn't be surprised he knew what was going on. Loreburn was a small town and if anyone had their ear to the ground it was Ed McAnulty.

Alex waited for Lara to reply but

when she didn't Alex said in her soft voice, 'Yes, thank you, things are going well. Would you like to have a look around?'

Lara opened her mouth to withdraw the offer but Ed was smiling, his whole face softening. 'That's very kind, if you wouldn't mind? Perhaps I could offer a word or two of advice? Not that I want to interfere . . . '

Lara tailed along behind them. She supposed it was good of Ed to come and apologise. And he did have one or two useful suggestions, not that she was going to let him know she thought so. She allowed Alex to do the talking, and was proud of her friend for handling the visitor so well. Her quiet voice and gentle manner seemed to bring out the best in Ed.

When he finally took his leave Lara said, 'What was all that about?'

'He probably just realised how much harm he could have done. It's good of him to come and own up, say he's sorry. He seems a nice man, really.'

Lara wouldn't have gone so far as to say that, but it was good to know they no longer had an enemy in the town.

★　★　★

The weather, which had been changeable during the last week of term, cheered up on the day of Mick's football tournament. There was a soft breeze and the sunshine was warm as he walked the fields, checking the condition of the pitches. Nobody else had turned up yet.

He groaned inwardly, wondering if the whole event was going to prove a huge mistake. What hope did he have of putting on a decent show with these kids? He had invited teams from as far away as Ayr and Kilmarnock, not to mention their local rivals, Stranraer. They would expect the tournament to be properly organised, which was never Mick's strong point. And they'd expect a decent standard of football — and behaviour. Neither of which he could guarantee.

The first person to appear was Steve, closely followed by Ryan. They were thirty minutes late, but Mick was just relieved they had turned up, especially Ryan.

'What's wrong?' he said to the boy, seeing the tense expression on his thin face. It made his spots stand out all the more.

'Nothing. 'S fine.'

'Nice to see they're as enthusiastic as ever,' said Steve, rubbing his chin. 'You sure the rest of them are going to show up?'

'They'd better. In fact, here are a couple now. Can you get them to put up the nets? I'll go and find the footballs.'

★   ★   ★

For the next hour Mick was too busy to worry, which was always the best way. He smiled to himself at the smart cars which brought the visiting boys. The

Kilmarnock team had even found enough money to book themselves a bus. Or maybe their local council was supportive?

Lara kept saying that there was money there to be tapped into, if you just knew how to get it. Perhaps he would take her advice and look into it when the new term started. But thinking of Lara just depressed him, so he determined not to do it.

His team looked almost smart in their yellow and green strip. There was an air of pride in the lads as they ran out, self-conscious before the crowd who had drifted in to watch. When he announced Ryan as captain he took the increased pallor of the boy's face as a sign of pleasure.

'Just make sure you win, OK?' he said, to hide the emotion he felt himself.

The first match was a disaster, losing four-one to Stranraer. But after that the boys seemed to wake up and start taking things seriously. The second match was a goalless draw. In the next match it was one-all at half time and the few spectators who had wandered up were starting to get enthusiastic.

Ryan made one of those darting runs from midfield that Mick liked to think he was himself famous for. Dinking around the opposing defence, he didn't even pause before taking his shot from the left hand corner of the box. He didn't score, but the move rallied his team and had Mick and Steve shouting themselves hoarse from the sidelines.

Five minutes from time it was still one-all and Mick was beginning to despair. If they could just win this one, they might make the semi-final. The team from Ayr were clearly going to win the tournament but Mick didn't mind, he just wanted his lads to do well, to have something to be proud of.

Ryan began a move forward again. He passed to Kyle and then ran the length of the pitch and was ready for the return. He was so quick he had left the opposition standing and now he had the chance to take a second touch, see where the goalie was and thump it into the far corner of the net.

The keeper actually got finger tips to it and for a moment Mick thought he'd kept it out, but he fumbled and the ball bounced over the line. Yes! Two-one with a minute to go. When the final whistle blew his team went crazy and Mick was nearly as bad.

* * *

His boys lost the semi-final resoundingly, but Mick didn't care. They were chuffed with themselves for winning a game, and only one boy had been red-carded. Pretty good going as far as Mick was concerned.

'You did all right,' he said to Ryan, cuffing him on the head. 'Now make sure you all stay for the final, OK? There might be something for you all at the end of it.'

There was a break for lunch before

the other semi-final and then the final. The boys were supposed to have brought packed lunches with them but most of them disappeared to the corner shop where Mick suspected they indulged in nothing more healthy than chocolate bars and coke. At least most of them reappeared again.

And then, just when he'd stopped looking out for her, because she'd only said she might come by, Lara turned up. She looked cool and beautiful as ever in white jeans and a T-shirt. He knew she had been working at Ladybank Row all morning, but her hair was smooth and glossy, her whole demeanour calm and controlled. That was what he loved so much about her — this ability to be understated, and yet beautiful. His spirits lifted another notch.

He gave Lara a hug, which seemed to surprise her. She pulled herself gently away, but she stayed by his side.

'You look gorgeous,' he said.

'Haven't you got things you should be doing?'

'This is my match off. Steve is taking my place as ref and I'm going to scout around and see what the standard is really like. Will you come with me?'

She smiled. 'As long as you don't expect an informed opinion.'

Mick liked the way people looked at him when he was with Lara. There was admiration and just a little envy. She was someone you could be proud to be seen with. He was delighted she had made the effort to come and see him here. He had to spend time glad-handing the other coaches, and keeping an eye on his boys, but he was always aware of her in the background. It made the whole day seem more worthwhile than ever.

* * *

Lara wished she hadn't gone to see the football tournament. It made her realise all over again what it was that so impressed her about Mick. His way with the youngsters, his persistence, his competence.

Everyone looked up at him, even the other coaches had seemed impressed, but he never seemed conscious of it, was never arrogant. He had been really pleased that she had turned up, which made it worse. How was she going to persuade him it was best if they remained just friends?

One good thing came from the tournament. Mick's football group were keen to do more training, buoyed up by their performance. This meant he was out of the house most evenings. Lara spent her days at Ladybank Row and although she couldn't actually ban him from accompanying her she did try to point out that this was their project, not his, and he had seemed to get the message.

Or so she had thought, until the Thursday after the tournament when she was happily noting progress on the installation of the central heating. A thud of footsteps below alerted her to a new presence and a moment later Mick appeared at the top of the stairs, jogging up as effortlessly as though he had not just run across town. He looked just as fit and scruffy and handsome as ever.

Lara gave him a small smile. 'Hi there.' She wished he hadn't come.

'Hi yourself. Everything OK?'

'Yes, of course. I didn't expect to see you here today.' That didn't sound very welcoming so she added, 'We're getting on really well. Ryan's around somewhere if you want to see him.'

'It's not Ryan I came to visit.' He smiled at her, green eyes twinkling, and she looked quickly away.

'Coffee?' she said, before he could say anything else.

They went down to the kitchen, empty save for the new sink and a stack of units waiting to be fitted. Lara set about making coffee for themselves and the plumbers, who had now moved to start work in Number Two.

'Do you want to go out somewhere tonight?' Mick said, as he poured milk into each mug. 'We can ask Alex if you want. Steve might come along if he's free.'

'Mmm. I'll just take these next door.' Lara didn't say what her plans were for that evening and when she returned he seemed to have dropped the topic.

'Anything I can do to help out?'

'No, no,' she said quickly. 'We're getting on fine. I'm sure you've got other things to do.'

'Seems like the only way to see you is to hang around here,' he said, smiling that smile.

She decided it was better to give in for now and they worked amicably for the rest of the morning, painting the newly plastered walls in the main bedroom. It gave Lara a great sense of satisfaction to see the way the house was coming together. And she had to admit that Mick was a good person to work with, thorough and not too chatty.

'I'm going over to see my parents on

Saturday,' he said out of the blue. 'I don't suppose you'd consider coming with me?'

'No. No, I don't think so,' said Lara. She felt caught out, not having had time to prepare an excuse. What had she been intending to do? Wash her hair?

'Why not?' he said bluntly.

Lara kept her back to him and concentrated on painting right into the corner. She was clearly wrong about him not being chatty. She thought he'd got the message that she didn't do families. 'I just don't want to.'

'They'll like you, you know. In fact they're dying to meet you.'

Lara wriggled uncomfortably.

'My sister says she's not sure you really exist. She says you sound far too good for me, and how come they've met every other girlfriend and not you?'

'I'm just not used to families that are so — interested,' said Lara feebly.

'It's lucky my parents've moved to Ayr, or you'd see just how interested they are. But they mean well. And for all my sister's complaints about them, the old folk are a great help with her kids. And she was there for them when Dad wasn't well. That's the way it should be, isn't it?'

'Hmm,' said Lara. She had enjoyed the week her mother had spent in Loreburn, but had seen nothing of either of her parents since then. They were busy in Devon and although they had invited her down no firm plans had been made. That was the way it always was, which was fine. She concentrated on pouring more paint into the roller tray and hoped that if she said no more conversation with Mick might languish.

She hoped in vain. 'I'd really like you to come,' he said quietly.

She stood the paint tin back on the floor and turned to face him. 'I don't know why.'

'I've told you, they've met all my other girlfriends. Why not?'

'Because . . . ' Because when they came to break things off it would be just one more factor to upset her. Better to finish now. She said abruptly, 'Alex and I are thinking of moving in here in the next couple of weeks. The house will be liveable as soon as the bathroom is finished.'

'You're . . . what?' He stared, eyes narrowed. 'Where did that come from? You're moving out because I ask you to visit my parents with me?'

'No, it's not that, don't be silly. We've been thinking about it for a while. We've really taken advantage of you, and now we don't need to. I think we should leave you in peace.'

'You're being ridiculous. You know I wouldn't complain if you stayed another six months at my house.' He put down his paint roller to concentrate the better on the conversation. She noticed the smear of white on his cheek, the hard look in his eyes. 'Come on, Lara, what's going on?'

'Nothing. I just thought, we've been seeing each other for a while, and you don't want to get too serious, so . . .'

'Who says I don't want to get too serious?'

Lara wriggled her shoulders uncomfortably again. She hadn't been looking forward to this conversation, but somehow she had expected him to accept the opening she was giving him. Now she looked longingly through the window, wishing Alex would come and interrupt them. 'But you don't,' she said quietly. 'You like to go out with your friends, and do all your usual things, you don't want to spend all your time with me.'

'It's not me who's trying to cool things, it's you. Come on Lara, admit it.' Now he sounded annoyed. 'If you want this thing to end, then say so.'

This was it, then. The end. 'I . . . ' she said.

'Well, do you? Want it to end or not?'

Lara felt as though the world was slowly falling to pieces around her. Now he had said the words out loud she knew this was the very last thing she wanted. But she had to do it. It was only fair to him. She opened her mouth to frame some kind of sensible reply, but her lips were shaking so much she couldn't speak.

Mick was glaring at her, hands on hips, waiting grimly for an answer.

'If that's what you want,' she said, in little more than a whisper.

'No, it's not what I want. For goodness sake, Lara, what is this about? I don't understand you. I thought you quite liked me, and now . . . '

Lara could feel the tears begin to roll down her cheeks. She hadn't meant it to be like this. 'I just think we should end it now. Before it gets . . . messy.'

'What do you mean, messy?' he demanded, running his hands through his hair so that it stood up in all directions. 'Look, I thought we had something here. I thought we maybe had something . . . different.'

'But you were going to end it,' said Lara. 'I know you were.'

'No I wasn't. If I wanted to, I would have said something.'

'Maybe you don't want to now, but you will soon.' Lara gave him a watery smile. She mustn't let him know how much this was hurting her. 'So better to end it now, OK?'

'No it's not OK. You mean you're going to break up with me now because you think that I'll break up with you at some unspecified time in the future?'

Put like that, it did sound ridiculous. But that didn't mean it wasn't true. Lara said, 'I'm sorry. I told you I wasn't very good at relationships.'

'I don't understand you.' Mick ran his fingers through the tumbled hair. 'Can't you just give us a chance? Why all this soul-searching?'

'Because that's the way I am,' said Lara sadly. She found a tissue and blew her nose. 'I'm sorry. I'm not light-hearted and easy-going like you. You said yourself I'm too serious. And . . . and I really think we should cool things off.'

'When did I say you were too serious? I think you're mad.'

'Then you're better off without me, aren't you?'

Lara could see that she had annoyed him, but she was doing the right thing. He hadn't contradicted her over the essentials, over the fact that they would break up one day so they might as well break up now. So she had been right about that all along.

'I'd better see how Ryan is getting on,' she said, desperate to get away from him. She ran down the stairs two at a time and hid herself in the little pantry, so she could sob her heart out in peace. There. It was done. Now the quicker she moved out of Mick's house and started her new life at Ladybank Row the better.

A Problem with Young Ryan

A few days later Lara woke to brilliant sunshine, totally at odds with her mood. It was going to be hot again. There was a haze over the town and the humidity was heavy in the air. She hadn't slept well and had a quick shower to wake her, but she felt no better after it. Then she climbed slowly into her car and drove to Ladybank Row. She parked in her usual place at the end of the cul-de-sac and climbed out. She smiled for the first time that morning. The sight of the houses raised her spirits, even today.

She stretched and nodded approvingly at them. Number One was starting to look different with its new front windows and the chipped-off harling. It wouldn't be long before she and Alex could move in. The front door was open which must mean Alex was here before her. Excellent.

They worked hard until about eleven, when Lara insisted on stopping for a coffee. It was whilst they were sitting on the battered garden bench in the little front garden that the police car drew up.

Lara and Alex looked at each other.

'We haven't been having any problems, have we?' said Lara, worried.

'Not as far as I know.'

Then their attention was caught by a movement at the far end of the row of houses. Ryan had been working on stripping out the fittings in number four. They had invited him, as always, to join them for coffee. As always, he'd accepted a mug but sloped off to drink it alone. Now it appeared he had seen the police — and run. Lara had barely realised it was him before his slim form vaulted the fence that hid the railway line and disappeared down the banking.

The policeman had clearly seen this too. One made a move to follow the youth but the other put a hand on his arm. After conferring for a moment they came over to speak to the girls.

'I presume that was Ryan O'Donnell?' said the older of the two.

'Ye-es,' said Lara reluctantly. She hated to think of Ryan in trouble. He had been working well and she was starting to have hopes of finding him a 'real' job once this was finished.

'How can we help you?' asked Alex in her pleasant way.

'We were hoping to have a word with Mr O'Donnell, but I suppose that's not going to happen now.' The man took off his cap and mopped his forehead. He suddenly looked much friendlier.

'Ryan's not in trouble, is he?' asked Lara. 'He's a good boy at heart. He's been working really well here.'

'We just wanted a word with him,' said the man again. 'I don't suppose you know any of his associates, do you? Or his brother, by any chance?'

'No, we don't,' said Lara honestly. She presumed Mick did but they had never discussed it. She knew Ryan came from a difficult background but she was determined to take the boy on his own merits.

'He's not doing himself any favours, running off like that.' This time it was the younger police officer who spoke, the one who had wanted to run after the boy. His foot was tapping and he seemed far less sympathetic.

'He'll be back,' said Alex quietly. 'Do you want us to try and get him to come down to the police station and see you?'

Lara stared at her. It had taken Ryan weeks to return to Ladybank Row after the problems with SEPA.

She suspected a possible brush with the police might put him off for ever.

'That would be good. You see what you can do.' The older police officer nodded approvingly.

After a few more words the two took themselves off and Lara was free to demand of Alex, 'Why on earth did you say that? We don't even know where he lives.'

'Yes we do,' said Alex. 'I gave him a

lift home one day when you had lent me your car. Shall we go and look for him now?'

* * *

Mick returned to Loreburn after only a couple of nights at his parents. It had been a mistake to go, although after that last awful argument with Lara he hadn't known what else to do. Now he was desperate to see her again and try to make her see sense.

The bus route from Ayr was a meandering one and it was early afternoon before he arrived at the Whitesands. The river was low, flowing sluggishly over the wide weir. It was a scorching day. He slung his backpack over one shoulder and prepared for the walk home. He decided it was good to be out, on his own. It might clear his head and help him decide what he was going to say to Lara when he saw her.

If he saw her. He had a sudden fear that she would have disappeared in his short absence. He quickened his pace. What a fool he had been to leave her alone. He should have stayed around, challenged her on all these weird ideas she had. At first he had been too surprised and, he had to admit, too hurt, to know what to do. Now, after only three days away from her, he knew he couldn't give up so easily. He missed her like a cold ache in his chest. He needed her. This cool contained beautiful woman had got under his skin like no one else. He knew now he was serious about her.

The only question was, could he convince her of that? Even if she felt the same way, and he was far from sure that she did, he suspected she would deny it to her last breath. For someone who was so brave and capable in many ways, she was a coward when it came to emotions.

The house was empty when he arrived. The girls would all be working over at Ladybank Row — wouldn't they? He ran upstairs and after a quick knock opened the door to Lara's room. He never normally went in here without her permission but he had to know if she had moved out. And she hadn't. The room was as tidy as ever, but even Lara left a few clues to her occupation, the book on the bedside table, the shoes neatly lined up beside the wardrobe. Heaving a huge sigh of relief he slung his rucksack into his own room and went back downstairs to plan his line of attack.

He switched on the kettle and began to glance through a copy of the Loreburn Standard, the local paper, which was lying on the table. Someone had folded back the front page and circled a small article, putting an exclamation mark in the margin beside it. If they hadn't, he wouldn't have given it a second look. Now he read it over once quickly, and then again more slowly.

'As part of their recent crackdown on house crime, police have arrested a number of men on suspicion of breaking and entering. Sergeant Docherty of Loreburn Constabulary reported there has been an upsurge in activity in this area and said the force are determined to crack down on it . . .'

Then there was a list of names, amongst them Sean O'Donnell. Mike had never met any of Ryan's family but he knew he had a brother called Sean. Oh no. Was Ryan involved in this too? He scanned the article again. There was no mention of Ryan's name or of minors being involved in the crimes, but Mick still felt a sense of foreboding.

Why had one of the girls circled the article if it didn't have a connection to them? He had to get over to Ladybank Row, fast.

He arrived to find a very unusual sight. Ryan was seated on the dilapidated garden bench and Lara and Alex were standing over him, both shouting. Yes, even Alex had raised her voice. And Ryan was saying nothing, not swearing back as he would have done at Mick, not turning and running as he had done so often when in trouble at school. He just sat there and took it.

As Mick drew closer he could hear what was being said.

'Don't you understand that if you're not guilty, you're not guilty?'

'It makes no sense to run. You have nothing to fear.'

'We'll come to the station with you. The sooner we go the better.'

'It's a good job you turned up today, we'd begun to think you'd run for it. Permanently, I mean.'

It was Ryan who spotted Mick first and the jerk of his head alerted the girls. Ryan looked back down at the ground, his face pale and possibly tearstained.

'What's going on?' said Mick to the boy. 'Are you in trouble?' He couldn't bear it if he'd involved the girls in trouble through introducing Ryan to them.

'I didn't do nothing,' said the boy.

'He's not in trouble, that's what we're trying to tell him,' said Lara, her voice loud with frustration.

'But he does need to go and see the

police. Running away when he sees them isn't a good idea. They want to talk to him about . . . things, and the sooner he gets it over with the better.' it was Alex who said this. She must feel strongly about it, to speak at such length. 'He just needs to make a statement.'

'I don't know anything. What can I tell them?' Ryan's words were belligerent, but his tone was defeated.

Mick couldn't help but feel sorry for him. 'They'll want to talk to you about your brother, I presume? I saw the article in the paper. You're not obliged to tell them anything that will get him into trouble, but hiding from them won't do you any good. Come on, I'll walk round to the police station with you now.'

'Excellent idea,' said Lara.

'And make sure you come straight back,' said Alex. 'You know we're relying on you here?'

'You don't want me back after this,' said Ryan sullenly. 'I just came to get my stuff this morning, then I'll be gone. I didn't do nothing, like I said, but no one ever believes me.'

'We believe you,' said Alex firmly. 'And we do want you back. We need you.'

Ryan looked at her, bewildered. Mick wondered if anyone had ever told him they needed him before. He patted the boy's shoulder. 'Come on, the sooner we get this over with the better. I won't leave you, I promise.'

Very slowly the boy rose to his feet. Mick was surprised to see how tall he had grown over the summer, still thin and gangly, but actually not too spotty. He was growing into a young man. If Mick had anything to do with it he would grow into a young man with a life to look forward to.

'Thanks, Mick,' said Lara. He was pleased to have her gratitude, but just now he had to concentrate on the boy.

Lara's Parents Speak Fond Words

Lara was beginning to dread phone calls. They never seemed to bring good news. So when Alex called her to the telephone early the next morning she came down the stairs sure that, whoever it was, she wouldn't want to talk to them.

'Lara, is that you? Sorry to call you at home during the holidays.' It was Hamish McIntyre, her Head Teacher and possibly the last person she would have expected to hear from.

'Er, no problem.'

'I hope I didn't wake you? I know that not everyone is up early in the holidays.'

'No, it's fine, I was up.' Lara was wracking her brains for a reason for his call.

'I was just phoning to remind you the closing date for applications for Mark

Frazer's job is the end of this month. I wondered if you'd like to come in and talk it over. You are going to apply, aren't you?'

For a moment Lara was lost for words. She had put the possibility of this job so firmly out of her mind she had actually managed to forget it. 'Oh. He's definitely leaving, is he?'

'Yes, as I confirmed at the end of term. I managed to get the job advert out pronto. I expect you saw it in the latest Educational Supplement.'

'I've, er, been rather busy.'

'How about coming in for a chat? Would later today suit you? I'll be in and around the school until four, always something here to keep me busy. Pop in whenever you like.'

'Yes, all right. Yes, I will.' Lara felt she was being rushed into something she might regret, but she wasn't sure how to get out of it. He was only asking her in for a chat, wasn't he?

'Excellent. I'll see you later.'

'More bad news?' said Mick, who

was already in the kitchen making toast. He was dressed most unusually in smart trousers with a shirt and tie. Lara didn't think she had ever seen him wear a tie before. He looked more handsome than ever, and very grim. 'It wasn't the police again, was it?'

'No. It was Mr McIntyre.' Lara made herself take her eyes off him. He looked so good, still a little wild and untamed despite the smart clothes. They had spoken of nothing other than Ryan's problems since his return home and it was important to keep it that way.

'What did he want?'

Lara frowned slightly. It really wasn't anything to do with Mick, now. Nor ever had been.

'He wants me to go and see him. It's about the Head of Department post. I told him I'm not keen but he still wants to discuss it.' She found she was willing Mick not to be annoyed.

He simply said, 'You should go for it. You'd be very good.'

'Like I was last time,' said Lara with a short laugh.

'Yes, probably,' said Mick, not looking up. 'Don't let that bully get the better of you. There's no-one's judgement I trust more than old McIntyre. If he thinks you can do it, then you can.'

'Oh. Thank you.'

He glanced up briefly. 'But don't let him bully you into it, either. It's your decision, Lara.'

'Yes,' she said, with a sigh. 'Yes, it is.'

She decided to call in at the High School before she headed for Ladybank Row. Otherwise, worry about Mr McIntyre would hang over her all day and she would get nothing done.

She parked her car in the deserted school car park and gave the heavy sky a quick glance. It was still warm, but dark clouds were gathering and it seemed the weather might be about to break. Alex would be pleased to have rain for her garden, even if it did prevent her making progress whilst it fell. Lara pulled on a light jacket and wished the dark clouds didn't have quite such a brooding look.

McIntyre was in his large office, seated behind the desk but dressed in light trousers and a casual checked shirt that made him look quite unlike her normal dapper headmaster.

After the initial pleasantries Mr McIntyre said in his abrupt way, 'Now, have you thought any more about Mark Frazer's job?'

'Well . . . ' said Lara, wishing she had given herself more time to think over her response. 'A lot of people would say I'm still a bit young for it. That was what they thought at my last school.'

'Fortunately I'm not a lot of people,' said the older man, smiling his small smile. 'I know a good teacher when I see one. Now, tell me what you think of the Humanities Department here and how you might like to take it forward. This is just an informal chat, you know, as I would have with any other candidate, but I'd like to hear what you have to say.

And any questions you have, fire away.' He leant back and waited for her to speak.

Lara gave up protesting. She didn't care whether she got the job. That being the case, she could launch into a description of how she would like things to be run in an ideal world, with no worry at all about actually having to translate this into reality.

Mr McIntyre nodded benignly and answered her questions. When Lara eventually left she found she had been with him for almost two hours. She couldn't remember half the things she had said, but that didn't matter, it had all been make-believe. Hadn't it?

'I can see that if you put your mind to this, Lara, you will do a really good job. And I'd like you to know I'm very impressed with the efforts you and your friend are making on behalf of young Ryan O'Donnell. It's nice to know we have teachers who don't shrink away from the problem youngsters.'

'We're not doing much. It's Mick, really . . . '

'You're sticking by him and that's what matters. Now, remember I'm counting on seeing that application.'

Lara groaned inwardly. His words to her were ominously serious. Why hadn't she just told him no?

★   ★   ★

Mick made his way across town to the offices of McAnulty and Sons. He was surprised that Ed had still kept the old name. It was meant to be McAnulty Brothers after their father had passed away, but the arguments between Steve and Ed had put paid to that. Mick wondered if Ed still had hopes of reviving the partnership. It had always been hard to know what was going on in Ed's mind, but all in all he wasn't a bad guy.

Mick had been furious with him about the asbestos, but when he heard from Lara of the apology he found he had changed his mind. Ed might be selfish and headstrong, but when all was said and done he was all right.

At least Mick hoped that was true. He was about to present him with an opportunity to prove it.

Unconsciously, Mick had dressed more smartly than usual that morning, as though a shirt and tie might have some influence over how Ed reacted. When he was introduced into the other man's office, he was glad of that decision. Ed was also dressed in a suit, sitting behind a massive dark wood desk, looking very imposing. Mick remembered how Lara had come here on her own, to beard the man in his lair, and was impressed all over again by her courage.

'Goodness, it's young Mick Jensen,' said Ed, indicating a chair on the opposite side of the desk. 'And what brings you here?'

'I was in the area, thought I'd pop in and say hello.'

Ed raised one very dark eyebrow and

Mick laughed. 'Well, that's not quite true. Actually, I came here to ask a favour.'

'Hmm,' said Ed, not encouraging. 'It's not to do with Steve, is it? I thought you'd have given up trying to get us to bury the hatchet.'

'I live in hope. But no, I'm not here about that.' Mick wished he'd thought this over a bit more carefully before rushing in. He realised he had no idea how to phrase his request. He tried. 'Have you got any vacancies at the moment?'

'What? Are you looking for a change of career? I have to warn you, building work is a lot harder than standing around on a football pitch all day.'

'It's not for me,' said Mick, not rising to the bait. 'It's for one of my young footballers. He's been doing some casual work for Lara and Alex and they're very impressed with the effort he's made. They're going to run out of work for him soon, and anyway he's not

283

really learning anything new. I wondered if you had something, may be an apprenticeship in the offing?'

'Apprenticeships? They're like gold dust. I can fill any I have ten times over, with good reliable kids, not someone who's been in all sorts of trouble.'

'Who said he'd been in any trouble?'

'I know the kid you mean. His brother's just been arrested? I'm not sure I want that kind of person on my books.'

'You weren't averse to twisting the law a little yourself, once upon a time, were you?' said Mick, beginning to be annoyed.

Ed paled. 'Look, I'm sorry about that. I've said so enough times, haven't I? I don't know what got into me. I think it was because I thought Steven had put them up to it and I was furious . . . I was a fool and I've held my hands up and said so. And paid the fine to SEPA, if you really want to know.'

'No more than you should,' said Mick, although he was secretly impressed with how remorseful Ed was. 'But doesn't that show you, you should give people a chance? Just because Ryan's brother is trouble, it doesn't mean Ryan is. I've been down to the police station with him and he's absolutely in the clear. But I'm worried if he doesn't find something to keep him occupied, maybe he'll be led astray.'

'Why should I take him on? There are dozens of other builders that might have an apprenticeship.'

'But I don't know them, and I do know you.' Mick paused, and when he sensed that Ed was weakening, said, 'I'll bring Ryan round to meet you tomorrow, how would that be? Then you can see for yourself he's basically a good kid.'

Ed tapped his desk thoughtfully. 'I think I'd rather see him on the job, see how he applies himself. You say he's still working at Ladybank Row? Why don't I call round there one day this week? I'll get the chance to hear what those two girls think of him, too. The one with all that long hair struck me as very fair minded.'

'Alex?' said Mick in surprise. 'Well, yes, I suppose she is.'

'A nice girl,' said Ed, giving a reminiscent smile. 'In fact they both are. Are you still going out with the dark-haired lass?'

'No, I've decided she's better off without me. I'm going to get Ryan off their hands then leave them alone.' Mick rose to his feet. 'I'll let them know you'll call by some time, shall I? Thanks for making the effort, I do appreciate it.'

'I haven't done anything yet,' said Ed.

Mick should have felt happy as he walked away. He had put the first step of his plan into action, to stop imposing on Lara, leave her free to get on with her own life. It had finally come home to him yesterday how many of her problems stemmed from him — the asbestos, the police calling round. No wonder she didn't want any more to do with him.

He had heard from Alex that she was going down to see her parents for the last week of the holidays, which was excellent news. He liked to think of her on good terms with them at last, and if she wasn't around then he couldn't weaken and try to persuade her to change her mind about him.

Before he was half way home the heavens opened and he was drenched to the skin. Typical. He hadn't even thought to bring a jacket with him. Lara would never be caught out like that.

★ ★ ★

Lara didn't know why she'd agreed to go to Devon. She had so much to do at Ladybank Row, which was practically ready for her and Alex to move in to. But her mum had been so excited when she phoned to say the spare bedroom was ready and somehow she hadn't been able to refuse. Her mum said her father was keen to see her. She doubted this was the case but she had had fun with her mum the week she had spent in Loreburn. It would be nice if they could maintain that new improved relationship.

She decided to take the train down and was pleased to discover that if she chose carefully she only needed to make one change. Maybe it would be easier to see more of her parents than she had expected.

They were waiting for her at Exeter station, her mother standing on her tiptoes in her eagerness to see Lara. And she looked happier than she had done in years, Devon obviously agreed with her. Lara gave her a proper hug before turning to give her father a peck on the cheek.

The house her mother had chosen was lovely. Lara wasn't surprised. Her mother had a knack with houses, even the many rented ones they had lived in over the years, a way of making them beautiful. Now she had one she could really make into a home and she was revelling in it. It was a medium-sized bungalow set amidst a well established garden, with views over the village down to the coast.

'It's lovely,' she said honestly, when she had been taken on a tour around. 'I thought you said it was a small place! It's not at all, it's really impressive.' Compared to Mick's place and the little Ladybank Row houses it seemed massive.

Elizabeth lowered her voice, 'Your dad did say he thought we might be taking on a bit much here, but it's so lovely, I couldn't resist. And, can you believe it, he's becoming quite interested in the garden! I'm hoping with that and golf to occupy him he won't be too bored.'

Lara shook her head at the idea of her immaculate father dirtying his hands in the garden, but decided not to tell her mother how unlikely this seemed.

* * *

The week passed by more quickly than she would have thought possible. She had expected it to be hard work having her father around all day, but somehow it wasn't. He was keen to explore the new countryside. In the bright English sunshine, so different from the searing heat of the desert, it was fun to do so. Who would ever have thought she and her father could have so much pleasure discussing rock formations on Dartmoor?

She hadn't even known, previously, that he too had wanted to study Geography and had only gone into Engineering at his own father's insistence. Why had nobody ever told her these things?

'Of course, you made an excellent engineer,' said his wife loyally.

'I enjoyed it, don't get me wrong. But you know, now I have a little time on my hands, I thought I might see what Geography courses the Open University have to offer.'

'As long as you remember Mum's counting on you to maintain the garden,' said Lara with a laugh. And then paused. Was she actually teasing her father? He was frowning so she added quickly, 'I'll look through the OU prospectuses with you if you like, I think it's an excellent idea.'

'Very kind,' he said, so she wondered if he was being polite or really wanted to involve her in the decision.

On the afternoon of her last day, they were taking tea on the little stone patio at the back of the house. Although there was still a lot to do to bring the property up to the Mason's high standards, they were already eating homemade cakes off beautiful porcelain plates. The tray even had a tray cloth. Lara had to smile. Her mother was amazing.

'It's been lovely having you here with us,' said her mother, returning the smile fondly. 'I don't know how long it is since the three of us were together for a whole week.'

Lara wasn't sure she could ever remember it. And yet it had gone so well.

Then her father said, 'What's this your mother tells me about the young man you're renting a room from? She says she thinks he might be rather keen on you. Is that right?'

Lara could feel herself going pale. 'Mick? Oh, no, we're just good friends.'

'That's a shame,' said her mother. 'He seemed such a nice man. His hair was a bit long, but I suppose that's young people today.'

'I'm sure he can't wait to have his untidy house back to himself once Alex and I move out.'

'I'm surprised you're going so soon. There seemed to be a lot still to do on those houses.' Her mother shook her head doubtfully.

'I'm very impressed by how much progress you've made,' said her father. 'I'll look forward to seeing it for myself when we come up. We were thinking of making a little tour of Scotland in the autumn, weren't we dear?'

His wife looked surprised and pleased.

Lara suspected this was something she had been trying to persuade Derek towards rather than something already agreed.

'That would be lovely. You could stay in Loreburn on your way north and again on your way back south.' Her father looked doubtful and she added, 'If you wanted to, of course.'

'That would be nice,' said her mother.

'We wouldn't expect you to put us up,' said her father quickly. He might be impressed with the progress he'd heard about at Ladybank Row but clearly didn't want to stay there. 'Your mother was pleasantly surprised by the standard of the hotel she was in last time. We'll probably give that another try.'

'I'll look forward to seeing you,' said Lara, and found that she meant it. It was amazing that after so many years her parents had mellowed towards her.

★　★　★

As they stood waiting on the platform the following day, Lara's father patted her awkwardly on the shoulder. 'You're a good girl,' he said. 'I hope you know we're very proud of you. I'm starting to think perhaps we've been missing out on something, being overseas for so long.'

Lara could hardly believe his words. She swallowed the lump that came to her throat. Perhaps they didn't think of their little surprise as a bad thing after all?

Her mother pulled her into a hug. 'Our precious daughter. I'm so glad we're home.'

Lara hugged her back, too moved to speak. She waved as the train pulled slowly away, realising with a jolt she would miss them. She leaned out of the window to call, 'Don't leave it too long until you visit!'

★ ★ ★

It seemed Lara was finally reconciled with her parents. This was really good news. And excellent progress was being made at Ladybank Row, especially now the girls had moved in. Mick wished heartily he could feel happier about it. He and Steve were having a drink on the last evening before he went back to school. Normally he was looking forward to getting involved in the hurly burly of the new term, but this time he didn't seem to have the energy.

'What are you so cheerful about?' demanded Steve.

'I'm fine. Lara and Alex have moved into Ladybank Row. A new start all round.'

'How do you feel about that?' asked Steve, sounding irritatingly concerned.

'It's nothing to do with me. It's not as though Lara and I are going out any more.' Mick felt a dull pain in his chest as he said the words.

'You've broken up with Lara?' Steve sounded angry now. 'I told you you'd hurt her. How's she taking it?'

'For your information it was Lara who broke up with me.'

'You must have done something to make her.'

With an immense effort Mick managed a smile. 'If I did, I don't know what it was. But I've realised it's for the best. I'm not what she's looking for. She's better off without me.'

Steve frowned. 'Did she say that?'

'Of course not. She said it was bound to end sometime and it was better to end it now. At first I thought I could make her change her mind. Now I've realised that it's best if I don't try.'

'You mean you only ever wanted a quick fling?' Steve's eyes were dark and he looked really angry.

'What's it got to do with you?' Mick couldn't believe that his own friend, Steve, who never went deep into anything, was getting at him like this. 'Just leave it, OK?'

He knew better than anyone that he had hurt Lara, and he would have done anything to avoid that. What she needed was to feel wanted. And he could have made her feel that. He knew now she was what he really wanted, not just for a few weeks but for ever. He swallowed abruptly at the thought of what he was giving up. He loved her, he really loved her. But he had come to see that she didn't love him back, and the best thing he could do was to leave her alone.

He remembered that haunted, hunted look she had had the last time they spoke, when she had taken the final box of her possessions away. He ached for the pain he had caused her. He couldn't do that to her again.

'Everything will be just fine.' Mick raised his glass to his lips and emptied it. 'Come on, let's have another. Then you can cheer me up by telling me how you're not getting on with that flat of yours. You know, the girls have done up a whole house in the time it's taken you to paint one room.'

'Two rooms. And they're paying people to do the work at Ladybank Row. Entirely different.'

Steve finished his own drink and

handed over the glass, evidently deciding there was no point in discussing Lara any more. Even he must be able to see that Mick would never be good enough for her, and that episode was best left in the past.

* * *

'What are you doing?' said Alex. She must have been surprised to see Lara with her laptop out. Lara was surprised herself.

'Tidying up my CV.'

Alex looked at her for a long time, frowning. 'For that job?' she said eventually. 'You're going to apply for it?'

'I'm not sure.' Lara sighed. She didn't know what had decided her to start work on her CV. She should really be thinking about lessons preparation, with school starting the next day. 'I might.'

'Your mum and dad will be pleased,' said Alex.

'Hmm.' Lara could think of someone who wouldn't be, but this was nothing to do with Mick. Actually, he probably wouldn't even be interested. He'd made no effort to contact them since they'd moved here. Which was exactly what Lara had hoped for, so she didn't know why she minded. Clearly he didn't even want to be just friends, never mind anything else.

She went back to her typing. She probably wouldn't get the job, but it would stop Mr McIntyre nagging if she applied. And it gave her something to do. The idea of going for promotion no longer filled her with sick dread. It didn't excite her either, but she supposed she could give it a go.

Then she would get down to some proper preparations for the new term. She and Alex still had a lot do to at Ladybank Row. It was going to be fun. Surely soon she would rediscover her appetite for life?

But the feeling of gloom continued to hang over her. She realised she was dreading the staff meeting on the first day of term. Mick would be there and she had no idea how she would react to seeing him again.

Part of her wanted desperately to see him, in the same way she kept going over memories of their time together, dwelling on them like a sore tooth. Maybe once the first meeting was over everything would be back to normal. Maybe none of the other staff would ask any questions, none of the kids would giggle and insinuate. Pigs might fly.

It took her so long to decide what to wear that, for the first time since she had started work, she arrived late. Thank goodness this was a non-pupil day. She was going to have to get her act together tomorrow. She pulled the linen jacket tightly around her shoulders and tried not to meet the eyes of all the people who turned to stare at her.

'Not like you to be the last one here,' said Marjory Jones, a Home Economics teacher. She shifted slightly to make space for Lara. 'Even Mick Jensen arrived on time . . . Oh. Like that is it?'

Lara kept her eyes on Mr McIntyre. 'I'm not very late,' she said, recognising his introductory pep talk from previous occasions. 'Better shush, he's glaring at us.'

Lara tried her best to concentrate on proceedings, but no matter how hard she focussed on Mr McIntyre, her eyes kept treacherously sweeping the room, desperate to glimpse a wild blond head. It took her nearly the whole meeting to spot him. He wasn't slouched in his normal seat beside Sandy Woods. But the main reason she hadn't seen him was because he looked so un-Mick-like. He had had his hair cut. Not the vague trim he had had before, but a shearing so severe all the blonde had gone, along with the curls. And he was wearing proper trousers instead of a tracksuit. True, his shirt was open-necked but he looked so like a normal teacher he had blended right in.

Lara swallowed quickly. Why on earth had he cut that wonderful hair? She didn't understand what he was up to.

As the meeting ended she headed straight over to him. It was best to get the meeting over with, wasn't it?

'Hi there,' she said quickly. 'I didn't recognise you. New look.'

Sandy Woods smiled. 'He looks like a shaved rat. Now we know why he kept it so long — to hide that ugly face of his.'

Mick smiled faintly. Lara didn't think his face was ugly, even with this stark hairstyle. His eyes were still that gorgeous green, his lips full and inviting. Except that now they just looked sad.

'Settled into the new house OK?' he said with false jollity.

'Yes, fine.'

'Alex OK?'

'Yes. Thanks.'

'Well, I'd better be off now. Lessons to prepare, you know. See you around.'

Lara stared after him. Something was very wrong. The problem was, she had no idea what.

An Emotional Confrontation

It was the pupils' first day back at school and it was raining with a steady, soaking drizzle that was such a part of Scottish life. Lara had heard that drizzle denoted low levels of pollution, but that might just be someone trying to put a positive spin on things.

The children seemed to feel much the same as she did. Resigned and unenthusiastic. They thronged the roads leading into the school grounds, chattering away, very few of them wearing coats. The classrooms would smell of damp wool today, but Lara preferred it to yesterday's echoing buildings, when all she had had to do was think about Mick.

'Morning, Miss.'

'Good holiday, Miss?'

'I saw you with Mr Jensen, Miss. Are you going out with him?'

'Are you? You're so lucky. I think he's dead cool.'

Lara tried to smile. She answered the questions about her holidays but not about Mick, and then began to take register. She had been given a third year class this year, which indicated Mr McIntyre really did think highly of her disciplinary skills.

All things considered, the first day didn't go too badly. She hurried home and changed quickly out of her smart skirt and blouse into something more suitable for working on Ladybank Row. She had no marking to do so early in the term, so could put in a good two or three hours on the painting. Alex had been on her own all day and would no doubt be glad of the company.

Alex, however, after professing herself pleased to see Lara and asking politely about her day, returned immediately to her digging. She said Ed McAnulty had been around again to chat about Ryan, and blushed as she spoke. She said this had held her up so she really had to get on.

Lara started the painting and put on the radio for company, but there was nothing she wanted to listen to. She actually wished Mick was there, at least she would have someone to argue with.

She finished painting one of the bedrooms in Number Two and rinsed out the brush and roller. Then she made a pot of tea and got out the application form for the Head of Humanities job, to check it over for the last time. She wondered how she would feel if she applied and didn't get the job.

She was pretty sure at least one of the other teachers in the department would apply. Malcolm Rowley was in his late forties and had been at the school for decades. Although there was nothing actually wrong with him she didn't think he'd set the world alight if he was appointed. But, as she thought it over, she realised she wouldn't be devastated either. He was a nice enough guy. He wouldn't intimidate her, wouldn't go all out to make her life a misery. And in the unlikely event she was offered the post herself she could see just how to involve him.

He had been running a History Club for years without any great success, but she knew he really loved it. Maybe if they changed it to include outside speakers, matched topics with the syllabus, that might work. They could even have some joint sessions with the Loreburn Archaeology Group, show the kids what their own area had to offer, that history wasn't just something you were taught in school. Lara smiled. It was good to be able to think like this, be positive.

She finished going through the form and put it neatly to one side. Then she gave in and allowed herself to dwell on what was really troubling her. Mick.

She hadn't managed to speak to him at school today. When she had passed him in the staff room he had smiled a vague hello and then ignored her. The pain he caused each time he did that didn't seem to be getting any less. She didn't understand him. Why was he being like that? It wasn't as if she had done anything to hurt him.

Had she?

A strange thought occurred to her. What if she had hurt him? Since going to Devon she had no longer felt convinced that love wasn't for her, that she couldn't take the risk. She had finally been able to see that her parents did love her, that she was important to them. That meant she was, actually, lovable.

So the question now in her head was: why shouldn't she take the risk? Why had she been such a coward for so long? Life didn't come with any guarantees but surely she was strong enough to give it a try. But when she had arrived back in Loreburn it seemed Mick couldn't wait to see the back of her. He'd even helped pack her boxes, to speed up the move to Ladybank Row. How ironic that when she was finally prepared to take a risk, Mick didn't even care.

Now she wondered if she dared hope that he did. That he had been hurt. That he wasn't staying away from her because he didn't want to see her. Might it not be, rather, because he did?

The very idea was terrifying. Thoughts swirled around in her head, but she could come to no conclusion. For minutes on end she felt crazily hopeful, and then she would remember his closed expression and be in despair again. How was she ever going to know?

She had to do something — but what? She was prepared to accept that she could change, that she might dare to love. Well, to be honest, that she already was in love with Mick Jensen and probably had been for months. But she didn't know whether she had the courage to tell him. It wasn't just the fear of rejection, it was pure, abject terror at revealing her deepest feelings to someone.

By the time she rose the next morning after an almost sleepless night she had decided. She knew Mick's early morning routine almost as well as her own, and if she was quick she could catch him before he left for school. She couldn't wait any longer. She had to speak to him.

It took Mick a while to answer the door and Lara stood in the cool morning air and wondered for the twentieth time if she was being a fool. Maybe he wasn't here. Maybe the last thing he would want was to see her. He had made that clear enough already, hadn't he? Cutting short every conversation, turning away from her smiles. What if she had got this all wrong?

And then the door opened and Mick was standing there in an old tracksuit, a piece of toast in one hand, looking as good as he had always done.

They stared at each other for a moment without saying a word.

Then they both spoke at once. 'I'd better be going.' 'Come in for a coffee.'

Lara hesitated. Wasn't this what she had hoped for, an invitation to go inside? She shrugged very slightly. 'OK, if you're sure.'

Mick didn't bother to answer. He stood back to allow her inside. The house was so familiar it hurt. The bags of sports kit sticking out from under the stairs, the milk carton left out in the kitchen.

Mick smiled faintly as he lifted the milk to smell it. 'I think this might be off. I'm useless at putting things away.'

Lara knew that. 'I have my coffee black,' she said. He knew that.

He pushed the back door open, as though the kitchen was too small for both of them. Lara sighed inwardly. This wasn't going well.

'It was really good of you to help Ryan out,' she said. 'Alex says he's really excited about working for a real builder.'

'He'll only be there on a trial basis, initially. After that, it's up to him.'

'At least he's getting a chance,' said Lara. 'And did you know that as a result of this Alex and Ed are getting quite . . . friendly?'

'Mmm,' said Mick, obviously not interested.

She took the mug he offered her. The silence was getting uncomfortable.

'Did you want to see me about something?' said Mick. He put his hand up to ruffle his hair, and then realised there was nothing of it to ruffle.

'I . . . ' said Lara. She put the mug down on the little formica table. She didn't think she could do this. Maybe if he had given her an opening, some sign of encouragement, she could have gone through with it. But how did you launch into a declaration of undying love when someone was checking their watch and looking bored? 'I've changed my mind,' she said. 'I think I should go.'

'Why did you come here?' he sounded tired.

Lara's nerve failed entirely. 'I made a mistake,' she said.

She marched to the front door, the door that had been her front door for so many months. She saw the little willow tree drooping under the drizzle that had started again, the crack in the letterbox, the scratched paintwork. Then suddenly she couldn't see any of it for the tears. She never used to cry. Now she seemed to fill up with any little emotion. Goodness, she had never even liked this house, why was she upset?

'Lara?' said Mick quietly from behind her.

She sniffed. He was bound to realise she was crying so she might as well get the whole thing out of the way. With her back to him she said, 'I came to tell you I thought we'd made a mistake, breaking up like we did.'

'I didn't break up,' he said. 'You did.'

'I came to tell you I made a mistake suggesting we break up.' She sniffed again and felt in her pocket for a tissue. She blew her nose and turned around to face him. 'I came to ask you to reconsider. I thought maybe we could give it a try again. But it's not going to work, is it?'

'Why not?' said Mick. His face

showed absolutely no expression.

'Because you don't want to.'

'I didn't say that.'

'But it's what you think.'

'No I don't.'

Lara stopped and stared at him. He was watching her warily from those beautiful green eyes. 'You don't?' she said in a whisper.

Then he put his arms around her and pulled her close, and she felt as though she had come home. She was crying and he was kissing her and then she was kissing him back. 'I've missed you so much.' He wiped her tears away with his finger. 'Don't cry.'

'I'm not crying.'

'You could have fooled me.'

'I'm happy. If . . . if you'll really let us have another try.'

'More than that,' he said, burying his face in her hair and holding her so tight it hurt. 'This isn't just going to be a try, this is going to be the real thing.' Then he pulled back and looked at her. 'For me, anyway. I love you, Lara Mason.'

He kissed her gently on the lips.

'Oh.'

'Is that all you can say?'

Lara was scared again, but scared in a good way, tingly all over. She said in a whisper, 'I think I love you too, but it's hard to get used to the idea.'

He laughed and swung her around and around. 'You've got all the time in the world,' he said.

And then he kissed her again.

THE END